"Richard has found a sponsor," she said

There was a long silence. Then Jason said quietly, "So your reason for entering into this arrangement with me is over."

"Oh, no." Virginia looked up quickly. "You don't think I'd back out just because my part hasn't worked out quite as expected?"

"I wasn't thinking in terms of backing out, Virginia," he said. "But circumstances have altered. I should quite ruthlessly hold you to the bargain—if I wished it."

"I don't understand. Do you mean you don't wish it?" Virginia had never felt anything like this chill of despair.

"Exactly. The truth is, my dear," Jason said calmly, "my wife and I have decided to make another attempt at reconciliation."

MARY BURCHELL
is also the author of these
Harlequin Romances

Many of these titles are available at your local bookseller.

For a free catalogue listing all available Harlequin Romances
and Harlequin Presents, send your name and address to:

HARLEQUIN READER SERVICE,
M.P.O. Box 707, Niagara Falls, NY 14302
Canadian address: Stratford, Ontario N5A 6W2

Yours with Love

by

MARY BURCHELL

Harlequin Books

TORONTO • LONDON • LOS ANGELES • AMSTERDAM
SYDNEY • HAMBURG • PARIS • STOCKHOLM • ATHENS • TOKYO

Original hardcover edition published in 1980
by Mills & Boon Limited

ISBN 0-373-02379-0

Harlequin edition published January 1981

CHAPTER ONE

THE light was failing absurdly early, the first few flakes of snow were falling, and Jason Kent was annoyedly aware that at least an hour ago he should have been in Oldmarket, twenty miles away.

All extremely aggravating, and all calculated to make a usually careful driver lose his temper and take risks. At least, that was the only way he could explain it to himself later, when he came to wonder how it was he had done such a stupid thing.

He distinctly remembered the long, grey road in front of him, the low stone wall that he seemed to have been following for miles, the sharp turn, which he took too fast, the second turning, as unexpected as the lorry which came round it.

He remembered the moment when he madly jammed on his brakes, the car turning a half circle and apparently trying to climb the wall. Then presumably the thing fell back more or less on top of him, because the world was blotted out with a terrific salvo of guns which spat fire.

His return to life was gradual, and accompanied by a pleasant impression of firelight and quiet and warmth. Then he moved experimentally and fiery pain shot through every nerve.

'Hell!' he said in a very weak voice.

By his side a girl got up and poured out something from a glass jug, and he watched her with interest. She was graceful, he decided. Not with the artificially achieved, willowy grace of the women he knew—but with a sort of primitive grace that suggested a certain amount of strength.

She came over to the bed and he was immediately assailed by terror—he, who had never been afraid of anything in all his cynical, worldly, rather disillusioned life.

'Don't move me,' he said sharply, with the recollection of that pain burnt on his memory.

'No, I won't. I'll just raise your head a little.'

She did so, and he drank eagerly. Then he leant his head back against her arm and looked up at her, studying her with a cool interest that was characteristic and not the result of shock or illness.

Under his gaze she coloured very slightly, her wide cheekbones were faintly flushed. Her mouth too was soft and full and very red, and her smooth white throat, with the little hollow at the base, had the same suggestion of strength as well as grace which he had noticed in her figure.

'What's your name?' he asked abruptly.

'Virginia Baron. I live here with my aunt.'

He saw no reason why he should ask about the aunt. Aunts did not interest him.

'I suppose I was brought in here after the accident?'

'Yes. You actually smashed into one of the stone pillars at our gate.'

'I apologise. Was there much damage?'

'It doesn't matter. You came off worse than the pillar.'

'Am I badly hurt?' He asked the question abruptly, but without obvious anxiety.

'The doctor said you must not be moved.'

'So I'm to stay in your house?'

'My aunt's house,' she corrected, but he brushed that aside impatiently.

'Are you going to nurse me?'

'I think a trained nurse will be coming in—at any rate visiting, but'—she glanced at him with a faint suggestion of shyness—'I dare say I shall sit up at nights sometimes. I can't imagine that my aunt will.'

'I hope not,' he agreed with fervour. Then he sighed impatiently. From the way the girl spoke, it all sounded very long and tiresome.

There was silence for a little while. Then he said, perhaps slightly piqued:

'You don't ask me my name.'

'No, I know it.'

'You do? Did you recognise me?' He seemed surprised, but not puzzled.

'Oh, no. Ought I to have done? It was just that you had your wallet in your pocket. Your name's Jason Kent, isn't it?'

He nodded. 'But that doesn't convey anything to you?'

'No. Are you famous, then?' The clear blue eyes regarded him with an interest that was not unpleasing, blasé though he was.

'I'm not exactly obscure,' he owned. 'Perhaps it's only in the business world that I'm so well-known.'

'Are you what's called a business tycoon?'

'Yes, something like that.'

'Then your being ill will mean that you lose a lot of business and money?'

'I don't know yet. I dare say.' He didn't know that his indifference to such a momentous question fascinated her, but he saw her eyes widen again.

'It must be nice to be so rich that you don't have to bother about anything.'

'There's no such state,' he assured her cynically. 'If you're poor, you bother about poverty. If you're rich, you bother about wealth. That's the only difference.'

She was silent for a moment. Then she smiled slightly and said:

'Well, I'd rather have to bother about wealth than poverty.'

He laughed, but frowned immediately afterwards because he found that it hurt him to laugh.

She noticed at once.

'Are you in pain?' She looked anxiously at him again.

'Yes. It hurts if I move, and I'm sick of lying still already. Talk to me,' he commanded.

'What about?'

'Yourself. Do you live here alone with your aunt?'

'Yes—Aunt Julia. I don't like her,' she said boldly.

'Then why stay with her?'

'Because,' she said, 'I'm one of the people who have to bother about poverty and not wealth. I have to be grateful for a good home where I can find it.'

'We-ell'—he smiled in his turn, but a trifle disparagingly —'why don't you go out and earn a living for yourself?'

'I've never had the slightest training for it. My aunt doesn't believe in women earning their own livings——'

'Are there really such people left?' he interrupted incredulously.

'Oh, yes. Surprising, isn't it?'

'What does your aunt visualise for your future, then?'

'I suppose she thinks I ought to marry.'

'Well, so you ought. You're lovely enough.'

'Do you really think I'm——'

'Lovely? Certainly.' His amused dark eyes confirmed that.

'Thank you.'

'Not at all.' After a moment he asked quite gravely: 'You're not—er—not engaged, then?'

'No. Not now.'

'Oh, you were once?' He seemed to think he had a right to ask these questions.

'Yes. Until this afternoon.'

'I dare say you'll make it up again,' he said carelessly.

'No. He wants someone else.' She made no bones about it. Just stated the unwelcome truth quite baldly, where another girl would have dressed it up with all sorts of explanations.

'He must have very poor judgment,' Jason Kent said gravely, and, oddly enough, he meant it.

'No, I don't think so.' The girl appeared to consider the point quite objectively. 'She's very pretty and lively—the girl he's marrying instead.'

'How remarkably generous of you.' He sounded cynically amused again.

'You don't bear her any malice?'

She shook her head.

'An amazingly impersonal state of mind. But then'—he studied her thoughtfully—'I think you're not exactly heartbroken.'

'No.'

'I suppose the marriage was just to be an escape from the aunt,' he said presently. 'Mind, I don't blame you.'

'It was partly that.'

'Only partly?'

'Yes——' Virginia hesitated. Then, perhaps because the strangeness of this conversation between them—alone in the middle of the night—tended to remove reserve, she leant forward suddenly, her elbow on her knee, her chin on her hand. 'You see,' she explained rather breathlessly, 'I have a younger brother. He's just seventeen.'

'How old are you?'

'Eighteen.'

'So? I should have thought less. But go on.'

'He too was brought up by my aunt. And, just as women shouldn't work for their living, she thinks boys always should——'

'Quite right too. I'm in agreement with her there.'

'Of course.' She brushed aside the interruption impatiently. 'But not just at anything—not just the first thing that will bring in money. They made him go into a City office and he's utterly miserable there. It isn't the life for him at all. He's a born artist——'

'Misunderstood genius, in fact?'

She didn't even notice the sarcasm of that, or if she did she ignored it.

'He *is* almost a genius.'

'We're all rather apt to be, at seventeen, my dear,' Jason said dryly. But this time the cynicism was not unkindly. It was absurd of her, of course, to be so agitated about her brother. It was always absurd to worry too much about anyone. But there was something compelling and rather touching about the intensity of her expression when she spoke of this boy.

'You think I'm a fool, don't you?' She was not exactly offended. Only disappointed and chilled that she had not made him understand her point.

'No.' He studied her reflectively. 'I should say you're anything but a fool. I should imagine, though, that our philosophies of life differ considerably. You're perfectly prepared to agonise over this brother of yours—probably make some absurd sort of sacrifice for him. Now I should never agonise over anyone—probably not even over myself, and certainly not over someone else. Nor should I make sacrifices for anyone. It isn't in my nature.'

'Not even someone you loved very much?'

'I've never loved anyone very much.'

'*Never?*'

'No.'

'How awful!'

'Is it?' He appeared to give that his serious consideration. 'I was rather fond of my wife once,' he offered at last.

She looked shocked at his words.

'I thought you were all for marriages of convenience,' he said softly and teasingly.

'Oh, no.'

'Only for yourself?'

'That's different.'

'It always is different for oneself,' he agreed. 'But may I not be allowed that sort of marriage too?'

'I can't imagine that you would need to. I mean—you've never needed money very badly, have you?'

'Good God, no!' He seemed scornful at the idea. 'It's always been there, and I always knew how to make more. But one strikes a bargain for other things as well as money.'

'Yes. Yes, of course.'

There was a short pause again. Then he said:

'Then you were going to marry this—this now vanished fiancé for money?'

'In a way, yes. Are *you* shocked?'

'Not at all. I can think of few things that shock me, and a business deal is not one of them. So you were selling yourself for your brother?'

'It was *not* selling myself!'

'It was, my dear. Just a little matter of a wedding ring added to the price.'

Virginia looked slightly sullen.

'I thought you said you were not shocked.'

'I'm not. I'm merely being accurate.'

She didn't seem to know how to answer that, so Jason said carelessly:

'He was very rich, this fiancé of yours?'

'Perhaps you wouldn't call him that. He was very comfortably off. I should have had money of my own at last, been able to help Richard as and when I liked——'

'And probably ruined him.'

'You're not very sympathetic.'

'I'm sorry.' He smiled at her without regret. 'But I have no doubt I know a good deal more about the world than you do. Broadly speaking, a regular job never hurt any young man yet—not even an artistic genius. But the means to sit around waiting for the moon to drop into one's lap—that can be fatal, even when provided by the most devoted of sisters.'

'Don't you think there are exceptions?'

'Of course. There are always exceptions. But we're all so apt to be the exceptions. I never met anyone who claimed enthusiastically to be the rule. Still, you know your own brother better than I, of course. Perhaps he's an exception. Perhaps he's wasted in a City office. And perhaps you're perfectly right to want to finance his artistic career. In which case, as you say, it's essential to have money. Couldn't he get a grant?'

She shook her head. 'He wasn't eligible.'

'So how are you going to do it now?' He regarded her with amused curiosity.

'I don't know. How *does* one find a considerable sum of money or even a regular income?'

'Is this a rhetorical question or are you asking me?' he enquired.

'Well—do you know the answer?'

'For anyone as lovely as you it should be moderately easy—so long as you're not troubled with scruples,' he remarked dryly.

'That's not much help!'

'Yes, I know what you mean. It's not a practical reply to an urgent problem.'

'No. Even suppose I hadn't—well, I hadn't any scruples, as you say. Suppose, for the sake of argument——'

'Purely for the sake of argument,' he agreed.

'That I was willing to do *anything*. I don't even know where one begins.'

'In Soho,' he said absently and literally.

'Where?'

'My dear girl, are you asking me to teach you prostitution in six easy lessons?'

She went quite white. 'I'm sorry.' Her voice had dropped to a very low note and it shook slightly. 'You wouldn't have spoken like that unless you thought me very—cheap.'

'On the contrary. It's the sort of flippant back-chat I'm used to among the women I know. I forgot that you were different—so much more sincere and—innocent, I suppose.'

She looked at him very seriously, not quite convinced.

'That's nice of you.'

'Oh—thank you.' He laughed. 'I'm afraid "nice" isn't quite the word. Aunt Julia, for instance, would withhold it, I feel sure.'

'Aunt Julia isn't any judge of men.'

'And you are?'

Virginia dropped her eyes, and that slight smile lifted the corners of her mouth once more.

'You're teasing me again, aren't you?'

'A little. Do you mind?'

She shook her head.

'Only I'm quite sure you shouldn't be talking like this. Hadn't you better try to sleep?'

'Perhaps. What did you say your name was?' he asked without opening his eyes.

'Virginia.'

'It's a lovely name.'

She didn't answer. There was a long silence. Then he said very sleepily:

'Did you say you were going to sit up with me every night?'

'No. I didn't say that.'

He smiled, but still without opening his eyes. It was too much trouble now.

'But you will, Virginia?'

'Perhaps. Go to sleep now.'

So he went to sleep.

There was silence in the room. The soft stirring of the

coal in the grate, the quiet breathing of the man on the bed
—but those scarcely counted as sounds.

Virginia sat very still. He must be really asleep now. He
hadn't spoken for a long time—not even with his eyes shut
and that attractive mocking smile touching his mouth. She
got up very softly, and crossed the room to look at him.
She had not been able to do that yet—not treat him to the
long, considering stare which *he* quite unblushingly allowed
himself—but her curiosity had not languished for lack of
being satisfied.

She even bent over him a little now, because when he lay
there in the shadows, it was not easy to see him properly.
And she wanted very much to see him properly. No one at
all like this had ever come within the narrow, conventional
boundaries of her life.

Even with those extraordinarily commanding dark eyes
closed, the face was an arresting one—a little less frightening
then, perhaps, because the unusually long lashes gave a
softening effect. But there was nothing soft about the
determined chin and the arrogant, faintly sulky mouth, even
in repose. She thought he looked a man who was used to
command and not in the least used to obey.

It was difficult to guess his age without seeing him move.
Thirty-five? Forty? Not less, she thought, for there was
more than a little grey in the thick, dark hair. He was evidently a man of some importance. He looked it—even without that careless reference to his being well-known.

It was strange that to-day, of all days, he should have
come crashing into her life—quite literally. When she first
heard the dreadful sound of the car smash that afternoon,
and then saw the men from the lorry bringing him in, she
felt it must all be part of the fantastic débâcle in which she
had found herself no longer engaged to Geoffrey, but just
thrown back into the futile, hopeless, futureless life with
Aunt Julia.

Her aunt was already extremely annoyed by the whole business and took it as something of a personal affront that the accident had happened outside her house.

Not that any feeling of Aunt Julia's went at all deep. That was the hardest thing to bear about her. She had apparently no capacity whatever for feeling. She had a mild affection for her huge Persian cat, who despised her openly, but that was the warmest sentiment that had ever been known to find harbour in her chilly heart.

Even now Virginia's mouth set angrily as she remembered the wastes of loveless discipline in which she and Richard had wandered in childhood. That was why she felt so fiercely protective now. It was the logical outcome of the days when she had had to shield a sensitive, woebegone little Richard from the harshness of Aunt Julia's rule, the nights when she had had to assure a snivelling, scared little creature that there was nothing to be afraid of in the dark— that it was silly of Aunt Julia to keep on urging him to 'be a man' when all the while he was only a small boy, but that she was there and he need not mind going up to bed without a light.

They were hateful days, she thought fiercely. Hateful, hateful, hateful! But she had always supposed that when they grew up things would change. To their envious, childish fancy it seemed that grown-ups were all omnipotent beings who did exactly what they wanted. When *they* grew up——

But they had grown up—long ago, as it seemed to her— and they had only changed one set of restrictions for another, one set of miseries for another. Richard was no longer afraid of the dark, to be sure, but, in place of that, was the ever-present wretchedness of being tied to a job he hated, doing work at which he was practically no good.

One of the other illusions of childhood had been that grown-ups had plenty of money.

Well—there was Richard now. Three thousand pounds a year. Probably not worth a penny more, she had to own, for she had no illusions about him, whatever the cynical man on the bed liked to say. It was all very well for him. Office life was his real milieu, no doubt. He probably actually employed dozens of Richards, now she came to think about it. No wonder he had shown little sympathy.

But, *pace* the business magnate, what was the use—what was even the sense—of spending one's days doing office work badly when one might have been painting pictures supremely well?

Her aunt didn't see it that way, of course. She just fell back on the comfortable generalisation that 'there was no money in art.' She was polite but very firm when Richard's art master at school had taken the trouble to call, and talk about 'quite unusual talent' and the advisability of a two or three years' training, 'perhaps finishing abroad.'

Virginia and Richard had held their breath with hope and fear at the time. So ridiculous of them, because, of course, there had never been the smallest, remotest grain of hope that such a thing would be allowed.

The very word 'abroad' would have scotched the whole project, even if nothing else had. One of Aunt Julia's favourite remarks was, 'I have never, I am thankful to say, been abroad. England is good enough for me.' And her tone always implied that she had escaped a major disaster by the narrowest margin of safety and the exercise of her own unrivalled common sense.

So Richard's business career was sealed.

Virginia, who would probably have enjoyed the un-domestic, comparatively carefree life of an office, was, in her turn, firmly debarred from such an unsuitable course.

'I am glad to say, my dear, that I am not so poor that I have to send you out into the world,' was how Aunt Julia put it. What she really meant was that it was more than satisfactory to have a general run-about at home.

As she looked at the man on the bed, Virginia experienced not only interest and curiosity, but a certain envy of anyone who was so arrogantly independent of action. He slightly despised her, she knew, for not having broken away from bondage, if, as she implied, she disliked being a slave.

She wondered what *he* would have done in the circumstances. Told Aunt Julia to go to hell, she supposed—and for a moment she was lost in pleasant speculation about Aunt Julia's probable reactions.

But independent gestures were all right if you could back them up with action. It was hard to assert your determination to start out on your own if you had about forty pounds in the world and no training for any profession or trade.

For a while it had seemed that Geoffrey was the absolutely golden solution. He was comfortably well-off, rather older than herself, and genuinely attached to her. He was not exactly the answer to any ambitious maiden's prayer, but Virginia was not ambitious. She only wanted to get away from her aunt in circumstances that would enable her to help Richard before the spirit and enthusiasm were ground out of him.

She had not put her views quite so frankly to Geoffrey, but she had at least admitted that she was not crazily in love with him. At that time Geoffrey saw nothing attractive in being crazily in love, and was perfectly satisfied with the comfortable, happy arrangement which their engagement appeared like to be.

Then Patricia Dent came along, and things changed completely. Geoffrey had old-fashioned ideas about 'doing the right thing by his fiancée,' but Virginia was neither blind nor stupid. She loved Richard, but saw no justice in sacrificing Geoffrey and Patricia to his artistic career.

She had had the whole thing out with Geoffrey that afternoon, and a rather uncomfortable but enormously relieved young man had presently left the house with the good wishes of his ex-fiancée wafting him on the way to his future bride.

Half an hour later Jason Kent's car had smashed into the front gate.

The man on the bed groaned a little and Virginia, who had returned to her seat some time ago, came back to the bed to look at him. He was still asleep, however, and the frown which had been there relaxed again.

Virginia went over the the window and pushed the curtain aside. Light was already streaking the sky, and the pale stars were going out one by one. From the leafless trees came the drip-drip of melting snow, and a few optimistic birds were stirring and twittering in the garden. It had not been a real snow-storm, after all. Just a light powdering of white, and now even that was disappearing fast.

She felt stiff and tired from her vigil, and she hoped it would not be very long now before someone came to take over the watch from her. He seemed so soundly asleep that one might almost have left him—but Dr Brown had been very emphatic about someone staying with him all the time.

The doctor had said some strange and frightening things about their dark, imperious visitor. She wondered with a sort of apprehensive pity what he would do if—well, if Dr Brown's more gloomy prophecies materialised. He was obviously a man of action, totally unused to the slightest restriction. But if what Dr Brown feared were true, there were going to be some pretty harsh restrictions for him in the future.

It was a rotten world, she thought—sleepy and pessimistic in the early morning light. Even overbearing business tycoons sometimes got a cruel knock from Fate.

CHAPTER TWO

WHEN Virginia awoke there was a bright daylight in the room, and a monotonous tapping was going on at her door.

'Jinny! Jinny!' said the voice of Aunt Julia. 'It's very nearly lunch-time.'

'Nearly *lunch*——' And then she remembered, of course, that she had been up all night, and so the invariable rule of seven-o'clock rising had for once been broken.

'All right, I'll be up in a minute,' she called out.

'And don't use *all* the hot water, mind. We'll need some of it in the kitchen, you know.'

Virginia muttered something unintelligible. It was entirely characteristic of Aunt Julia's household that there was never enough hot water. You could have a really hot bath and no hot water in the kitchen, or a tepid bath and a moderate supply of hot water in the kitchen. But you could *not* have hot water upstairs and downstairs. Aunt Julia didn't see any reason why you should. She even spoke of households where there was a constant supply of hot water, as though they hovered on the brink of vicious indulgence. What happened in her house was good enough for anybody.

Virginia got up, had her tepid bath and dressed just in time for lunch. It was still a very serious fault to be late for any meal. Besides, she was hungry by now, having missed her breakfast.

It was a good meal, like all the meals in Aunt Julia's house. She herself had a keen appreciation of food, and the result was fortunate for those who sat at her table. But this meal was fated to end less happily. It was only a few minutes before Virginia's ringless hand was noticed and commented on.

'Have you lost it?' Aunt Julia's deep voice held such a note of disaster that it might have heralded the Second Coming.

'No. I'm not engaged any more, that's all.' It was not a well-chosen reply, Virginia knew, particularly the 'That's all' at the end. Her aunt would think that distressingly flippant.

'When, Jinny,' asked Aunt Julia, 'did this happen?'

'Yesterday afternoon, Aunt Julia.'

'And you didn't see fit to tell me until now?'

'Well, in the excitement of the accident I almost forgot and——'

'He—he jilted you?' Aunt Julia brought out the horrid word as though it were breakable.

'Not exactly. No—certainly not. I knew he was in love with Patricia Dent. It would have been idiotic to have gone on with things—and very wrong, too. I told him I knew how he felt——'

'*You* told *him*?'

'Well, of course.'

'I don't understand,' Aunt Julia said bitterly, as she helped herself to a large portion of pudding. 'I don't understand at all. Either your attitude or that of Geoffrey. You speak of this—this making and breaking of engagements as though it were of less importance than a decision about a day's picnic. And you seem to imply that Geoffrey—whom I had always considered until now to be steady and serious-minded—shares your lightness of outlook.'

'Well, not exactly, Aunt Julia.' Virginia felt the discussion was doing less than justice to Geoffrey. 'It really *would* have been all wrong for him to marry me, feeling as he did about another girl. And since we found out in time, the only thing was to rearrange things. It's really just common sense.'

'I don't think I wish to discuss the matter any further, Jinny.' Aunt Julia could make this cowardly form of escape with more dignity than anyone else Virginia knew. 'I'm disappointed in Geoffrey, and I can't say I'm pleased with your attitude.'

Virginia escaped upstairs.

Her light tap on the door was answered almost immediately by a weak but slightly interested, 'Come in.'

She went in and Jason greeted her at once with a not very agreeable:

'Oh, it's you at last. Why didn't you come before?'

She detected the irritation of a sick man in that, and smiled as she replied:

'Because I was asleep.'

At first that only drew an unfriendly stare. Then he smiled slightly and his dark, shadowed eyes looked less weary.

'How are you feeling?'

'Damnable.'

'Oh, I'm sorry.' She became serious at once.

'You needn't be.' He sounded impatient

'Have you been asleep all the time since you left me?' he asked.

'No. I had lunch. Oh, and a talk with Aunt Julia.'

'What does she think of the broken engagement?'

Virginia was surprised that he bothered to remember so much of what she had said last night. He spoke as though he knew her aunt, and could appreciate to the full how tiresome she would be about such a matter.

'Theoretically, she's very shocked.'

He laughed.

'And actually?'

'Oh, it's impossible to tell. I don't care very much.'

'My dear girl! I begin to understand why you acquired that fiancé with such determination.'

She flushed again.

'That isn't a very nice way of putting it.'

'No,' he agreed carelessly. 'But I'm not a very nice man. I think I told you that before.'

She was silent.

'Are you offended, Virginia?' He spoke softly, and for the first time she noticed what an attractive speaking voice he had.

'A little, yes.'

'Because I tease you?'

'Because you make me feel that if I knew a little more about the world, I should probably find you were being almost offensive. It's just that I'm not used to your kind of conversation and I think you often mean to be unkind.'

He considered that.

'It would be a very poor return, wouldn't it?'

'For what?'

'For your kindness to me.'

'Oh.' She smiled reluctantly.

'Did your fiancé ever tell you that you have a most beautiful smile?' he said.

Virginia looked at him gravely.

'Is this another verbal trap or just a straight question?'

'Oh, come, there's nothing very obscure about that, is there?'

She hesitated.

'Well, he didn't. Geoffrey never said things like that.'

'He didn't? Strange fellow.'

'Why? Do *you* go about telling women they have beautiful smiles?'

'Certainly not. Most of them haven't. But if you were my fiancée I should see no reason whatever for keeping a palatable truth from you.'

She laughed reluctantly. It was difficult not to when he talked like that.

'Well, it was nice of you to let me into the palatable secret,' she said boldly.

'I think I can hear a car outside. It must be the district nurse. The doctor said she would call.'

'I'm sorry.'

'Are you? Why?'

'For the very obvious reason that you're much more interesting company.'

'Oh.'

She realised that, for some reason, that remark from him gave her much more pleasure than anything Geoffrey had ever said to her.

'Wait a moment. It may not be the nurse. I'll look out and see.'

She went out of the room, and leant over the banisters, so that she could see into the hall below.

Aunt Julia was in the doorway of the drawing-room rather like royalty receiving, ushering a stranger across the hall. Quite the loveliest and most overwhelming stranger Virginia had ever seen.

She caught a general impression of wonderful furs, a tiny but exquisite head crowned by Titian hair, a delicate, proud, beautiful little face, and a soft but penetrating voice saying something about 'Mr Kent'.

Then the drawing-room door closed behind the visitor.

Slowly Virginia went back into the bedroom.

'It wasn't the nurse,' she said.

'No?'

'But I think it was a visitor for you.'

'So? Man or woman?' Jason didn't seem specially interested.

'A woman.' That didn't seem quite the word to describe the exquisite creature downstairs.

'Really?' He seemed surprised. 'You didn't catch her name?'

'No.'

'Was she very lovely?'

'Yes.'

'And very beautifully dressed?'

'Oh, yes.'

'I expect it's my wife,' he said without interest.

'Your—wife?' Even her realisation that he was a very unusual person didn't quite reconcile her to his odd way of speaking of his wife.

'Yes.'

With a sudden little flash of indignation, she exclaimed: 'Do you think you ought to talk like that?'

She saw extreme astonishment and then extreme amusement flash into his eyes.

'Probably not,' he agreed, and waited to see what she would do about it. But she didn't do anything. For one thing, she could hear Aunt Julia's voice as she obviously led the way upstairs.

Feeling suddenly very nervous, Virginia stood up as the door opened. The lovely visitor came in first, and then Aunt Julia.

'Jason, darling! However did you come to do this?' The voice was so soft and sweet, but somehow there was an undercurrent of displeasure which Aunt Julia herself could not have bettered.

'Hello, Ginette. The usual way. Speeding.'

'My niece,' Aunt Julia said, with an air of putting first things first. 'Mrs Kent.'

Without kissing her husband, or in any way expressing affection or concern, Ginette Kent turned to Virginia and held out her hand with a charming smile.

'I hear you've been acting as night nurse for my husband. It's very good of you.'

'Oh, no, there wasn't any work attached to it. And he's a very good patient.'

'Is he?' Mrs Kent laughed prettily. 'I'm glad to hear you're a good something, Jason.'

'I expect you would like to have a talk with your husband alone,' said Aunt Julia, and Virginia had the most curious impression that really nothing was further from the wishes of either husband or wife.

However, Mrs Kent gave her charming smile once more and murmured suitable thanks.

'Come, Jinny.' Aunt Julia spoke as though Virginia were an inquisitive child who would certainly have remained if left to her own devices.

Virginia noticed with a sort of gratified amusement that Jason Kent winced openly at the hideous abbreviation of her name. Then she followed Aunt Julia out of the room.

Downstairs Aunt Julia, true to her usual policy, said nothing at all, as though the whole subject could be entirely ignored so far as she was concerned. Virginia knew better than to discuss their glamorous visitor. They sat in silence.

Virginia found herself wondering just what was happening in the room upstairs. She had never seen any husband and wife have such a curiously indifferent air towards each other, and yet, individually, they were singularly attractive people.

Somewhat to her shamed amusement, Virginia even found herself 'taking sides'. Jason Kent might have his faults, and he was, she felt sure, a difficult man to live with, but something about the cool tone, the charming but unvarying expression, the faintly hard set of the mouth, made Virginia decide that at least half the blame—if not more—rested on Mrs Kent's pretty shoulders.

Less than half an hour after she had gone into her husband's room, she came downstairs again. Aunt Julia hurried to the door of the drawing-room and offered her tea.

Rather to Virginia's surprise, the invitation was accepted, and Ginette Kent came slowly into the room. She looked—there was no other expression for it—mildly annoyed by the whole proceeding. Virginia thought what an extraordinary reaction this was for a woman whose husband had just been seriously injured.

Not a single line of anxiety marred her beautiful face, not a shade of her delicate colour had faded. It was almost uncanny.

'And how did you find him?' Aunt Julia was enquiring.

'I suppose it might be worse.' She sighed impatiently. 'I was really expecting that he would be only half-conscious and unable to talk at all. But of course, it's a dreadful business.'

'Dreadful! Dreadful!' Aunt Julia agreed, with ten times the expression that their visitor put into the word.

'Perhaps it isn't so bad as Dr Brown thinks,' suggested Virginia.

'Well, of course, one must hope,' agreed Mrs Kent conventionally. 'His whole attitude won't improve matters, I'm afraid.'

'His—attitude? What do you mean?' Virginia's voice sounded a little sharper than was polite.

'Well, he practically refuses to believe——'

'You *told* him?' For a moment Virginia forgot that this woman was a guest and a stranger. 'You—you couldn't have done anything so awful.'

'My dear'—Mrs Kent gave a sweet, displeased laugh—'he had to know some time.'

'Oh, yes, but not now—not until he's better and can stand it. Besides, there may be a chance——'

'Jinny!' Aunt Julia's voice broke in with astonishment and displeasure quivering in every syllable. 'Aren't you forgetting yourself in a most strange manner? What Mrs Kent says, or does not say, to her husband, is surely *entirely* her own business.'

Virginia wanted very much to say it was the business of the husband, too. But she had to keep silent, of course, to look down with some appearance of shame and murmur an insincere, 'I'm sorry.'

She found she was actually quivering with feeling. It surprised her. She had not been moved to the depths like this since the days when Richard was small, and her fierce protectiveness had constantly been called in to being in his defence. That was how she felt now—fiercely protective. Though, heaven knew, that cynical, wordly man upstairs could probably protect himself.

But she wanted terribly to go to him. That, too, was absurd, because he probably didn't want her there in the least. He had other things to think of now that his charming informative wife had been. But she wanted to go, all the same. She had the feeling that he was most desperately, tragically alone.

In answer to Aunt Julia's grimly expressed hope that she would come again whenever she wished to, Mrs Kent returned polite but vague thanks. Then she went out to the car which was waiting at the gate, and drove away without even a backward glance at the smashed pillar which marked the scene of her husband's accident.

'A very—very *reserved* woman,' commented Aunt Julia when she had gone.

Virginia didn't wait to hear any more. Without a word, she went out of the room and up the stairs. It was at least as likely as not that Aunt Julia would call after her to know what she was doing, just in case Virginia were anticipating any independent action. But by going slowly and giving as convincing an air of preoccupation as she could, Virginia escaped question this time. Which was interesting—because she *was*, for once in her life, bent on independent action. With only the lightest tap on the door, Virginia went into the guest room, closing the door behind her.

He was lying there with his head turned away, either asleep or staring at the pattern of the wallpaper. He didn't move as she came into the room, but when she crossed to the side of the bed, he turned his head and looked at her.

There was no question of his having been asleep. Those dark, shadowy, restless eyes were tragically wide awake.

She felt so sorry for him that, for a moment, she could think of nothing to say, but just took the rather slack hand that was lying on the coverlet. Even that brought no response at first. Then the cold fingers curled nervously round hers. He looked down at her hand and said harshly:

'Is it true? Shall I really not walk again?'

'It isn't certain. There's only a grave danger of it. Didn't your wife explain that?'

The grip on her hand tightened painfully.

'No,' he told her a little breathlessly. 'No, she didn't tell me that. But then she wouldn't.'

'Perhaps she didn't quite understand.'

Virginia felt bound to make that statement, improbable though it seemed, and the short, unamused laugh with which he dismissed it told her his opinion.

She sat down by the bed, her hand still in his, because he was holding on to it with a grip which suggested that he needed some sort of reassurance.

'Virginia, will you tell me just what's happened. I think I should believe what you told me.'

'I hope so.' She smiled at him. But he only said impatiently:

'It doesn't follow. Most people lie about illness, either from a mistaken sense of sympathy or else from—spite.'

'I won't lie to you. But I only know just what Dr Brown said about you. In his opinion it isn't possible to tell yet how far you've injured your spine. It might mean that—that you couldn't walk again. Or it might mean complete recovery.'

'He *said* that? You're not adding that last bit on your own?'

'I told you I shouldn't lie to you.'

'No. No, of course not.' He seemed suddenly dreadfully tired from the nervous strain, and his eyes closed.

Virginia leant forward anxiously and very gently pushed back the heavy dark hair which had fallen forward over his forehead. The movement seemed to astound him, for his eyes opened again at once, and he looked almost startled.

'I'm—sorry.' She felt strangely confused.

'No, that's all right.' There was silence for a few minutes. Then Jason said abruptly:

'This Dr Brown—he's only a country practitioner, I suppose?'

'No. He's something of a specialist in spinal injuries, as it happens. He goes up to Town twice a week, and I think has a consulting-room somewhere near Harley Street.'

'That doesn't necessarily mean anything,' was the rather disagreeable reply.

'You mean you want another opinion? Some specialist you know of?'

'I don't know of anyone personally,' he explained impatiently. 'I've never been ill in my life before.'

'It's always extra dreadful the first time, I imagine. There's something so frightening about it, apart from anything else.'

'Thanks, Virginia. You have a knack of restoring my self-respect every time I begin to wonder if I'm a nervous, self-pitying coward.'

'You're not that in the least,' she said in a matter-of-fact tone. 'And anyone would have been bowled over by what you've just been told. Particularly——' She hesitated.

'Particularly?'

'As you heard it first without any—any modification attached.'

'Oh—you mean Ginette's frank way of putting things?'

'She might at least have let you know there was a little hope.'

'No—oh, no. She wouldn't see it like that. I think she was interested to observe the result of real disaster on me.'

'Oh, surely—— Don't you think that perhaps—perhaps you imagine a little—being ill and——?'

'My dear girl'—he brushed the protest aside—'you must surely have seen that there's a singular—lack of sympathy, shall we say, between us.'

'Yes, but to do anything so desperately unkind——'

'Ginette is unkind. In fact,' he added thoughtfully, 'I think she's the most detestable woman I know.'

CHAPTER THREE

THERE was a profound silence after this last remark.

Presently he stole a look at Virginia as she sat there beside his bed. Then she knew he must have recovered slightly from the terrible blow he had received, because he smiled maliciously and enquired:

'Have I shocked you once more, Virginia?'

'Well—if you want me to be frank——'

'Oh, I do.'

'I don't think that kind of remark is amusing.'

'Even if it's true?'

'Yes—even then. After all, you promised certain things when you married your wife——'

'No. We were married at a register office.'

'It doesn't make any difference.' She flushed slightly at the amused interruption. 'Just by marrying her you *implied* certain things. If you've changed now——'

'But suppose she changed, Virginia?'

'Are you trying to put all the blame on her?'

'No, certainly not. I dare say I turned out much less easy to live with than she'd expected. But'—he smiled straight at Virginia—'if I may say so, without shocking you, the disappointment was not all on one side.'

'Don't you think those things are—are for private regret rather than——'

'Broadcasting to a sympathetic nurse? Yes, you're right, of course, my severe little critic. It was rather wicked to say that to you. I probably shouldn't have said it to anyone but you.'

'But why—me?'

Jason slightly narrowed his dark eyes as he smilingly studied her.

'Perhaps it's just that I'm in a weak foolish mood after the accident and want to babble to the nearest hearer.'

'You don't give that impression at all,' Virginia informed him seriously, and at that he laughed again—slightly, but with genuine amusement.

Then, after a moment he spoke again, seriously this time, and with a suggestion of something like nervousness— except that one could not really credit the idea of nervousness in anyone so overwhelming.

'Did this Dr Brown say anything about how—long it might be before we could know——'

His voice trailed off, but his eyes asked the rest of the question. And at that her heart softened towards him again.

'He couldn't tell. That's the worst part of it. You see, I'm trying to be quite truthful still, although it isn't a nice truth. He thought in two or three months——'

'*Months*, Virginia?'

'I'm afraid so—yes.'

He made a slight face and tried to pass the whole thing off with a touch of cool bravado, but she saw he was terribly shaken.

'It looks as though I shall have to learn some sort of patience.'

'I'm afraid so.' She looked at him very sympathetically. 'You're not a very patient person, are you?'

'No. Perhaps I've never had to be and now I must, per-force. I must take care not to become warped.'

'I don't think it's likely.'

'No? I don't agree with you. I can imagine there's already enough cynicism and ill nature in my make-up to set me well on the way.'

'Oh, no. You have too much common sense and—balance for that.'

'I hope you're right.' He half closed his eyes, but con-tinued to look at her through his lashes. 'Is it by artful

intention or natural tact that you so often say just the things
I want to hear?'

'I—don't know what you mean.' Virginia was confused
again, guessing that this was partly teasing, but not able to
decide how much of it was. 'There isn't any "artful intention" behind it.'

'Sure?'

'Of course. Why should there be?'

'Only that I sometimes remember you still haven't
settled your brother's problem—and I'm a very rich man.'

It was a few seconds before the full import of that sank in.
And then she didn't pause to decide whether Jason was
serious or teasing. An angry flame of colour ran all over her
neck and cheeks, and without a word she got to her feet.

He watched her with amusement not untinged with
dismay, and seemed to await her answer with mocking
anxiety.

But no answer came. Still without a word, she went out
of the room, and even his rather perplexed 'Virginia?' did
nothing to alter her decision.

She was furiously angry and bitterly dismayed, too. Well,
that was what came of being too frank with people—interesting yourself in their affairs instead of minding your own
business.

He thought her a cheap and very clumsy schemer, over-
sympathetic because she had some idea of getting money out
of him. The mere thought of it made her writhe.

Had she given that impression? *Had* she said or done
anything to justify such an idea? She felt too miserable and
humiliated to answer that question herself. She only knew
that she never wanted to run such a risk again—never
wanted to talk to the man again, come to that. And she
was determined, at least, that she would not sit up with him
that night. Her aunt could arrange what she pleased.

She tried to arrange it, of course, exactly as she pleased—

which was that Virginia should do any sitting up there was. But with unusual determination she insisted that she had a bad headache, that she must go to bed, and she was sorry, but this night at least she must be let off.

It gave her a slight, malicious satisfaction to find that Aunt Julia, divided between curiosity and necessity, was prepared to take on the vigil. And, as she got into bed that night, she thought bitterly:

'Let him confide his marital troubles to Aunt Julia, and see how *she* likes it!'

But apparently he confided nothing at all to Aunt Julia because, sleepy and disappointed, she reported the next morning that 'he had slept part of the time, and scarcely uttered a word, poor man,' even when he was awake.

She drew the most pessimistic conclusions from this.

For Virginia, the really important event of the morning was that she received a letter from Richard. He was not a frequent or a regular correspondent, which meant that, between letters, she was apt to worry about him in an ever-deepening degree as the silence continued. She wished Aunt Julia would get a phone installed.

The letter this morning was despondent in the extreme. He saw no future ahead but the grey futility of his present position, and sometimes he wondered 'if it were worth while going on.'

Virginia's heart came into her mouth at this slightly melodramatic statement. What did Richard mean by that exactly? Nothing—surely nothing—desperate? There was never any knowing with him. He was such an impulsive, delicately balanced person. That was his crassly idiotic upbringing, she always used to assure herself, not wanting to admit that her darling had any really fundamental fault.

She made a somewhat clumsy escape from the house by offering to do the day's shopping in the village, a mile away. Usually Aunt Julia preferred to do this herself, as she suspected every tradesman of a deep-laid plot to defraud her. But to-day, as it was raining hard, she yielded the task to Virginia.

Pulling on a raincoat which, by some oversight of Aunt Julia's, happened to be extremely becoming, she set off through the rain.

It was pleasant to get out of the house, she thought, even into the rain. There was always something free and lavish and unrestricted in the open air, and one never felt that at home. As she trudged along the wet lane, her basket over her arm, her thoughts turned first to Richard.

Something *must* be done soon. If the engagement to Geoffrey had not foundered, she could probably have hurried on her marriage, and then she would soon have been in a position to help her brother at least a little.

Now that was all over. It was no good moaning about it. Fortunately, at least she had never represented it to Richard as a concrete plan. There would have been something too crudely mercenary about that, and she didn't want him to know that she had ever had such thoughts on his behalf. But there had seemed very little harm in just hugging the thought to herself: 'When I'm married I can help Richard. Geoffrey won't mind. I shall do this and this and this.'

But unfortunately there was now Patricia Dent, and so everything was changed. Just as that hateful man had implied, she would have to 'find something else.'

She wondered then how *he* was, whether he had loathed Aunt Julia, whether he were a little chastened by the experience of being deserted, whether his remark had been meant to be quite so cutting and unkind as it had sounded.

Not that it mattered, of course. He would go away quite soon probably—as least, as soon as Dr Brown decided that he could be moved by ambulance—and then she would never hear of him again. And a good thing, too.

It was on her way back, when she was within twenty

yards of the gate, that the energetic-looking man in the raincoat stopped her. He greeted her politely and said:

'Excuse me, but wasn't it about here that there was a bad accident a few days ago?'

'Why—yes. Just there by the gate. You can still see the damage to the pillar.'

'Oh, yes, to be sure. Do you—happen to know the people of the house?'

'I live there.' Virginia looked at him in some surprise, particularly as this information seemed to interest the man enormously.

'Oh, you *live* there? That's very interesting. A very unnerving experience for you.'

'Well, I didn't actually see it happen. But—yes, it was upsetting, of course.'

'And the—the victim was brought into your house, I suppose?'

'Yes.' She wondered very much why he wanted to know all this, and thought it was extraordinary how much some people could interest themselves in the concerns of others. If she could have passed him, she would. But he was standing squarely in front of her on the narrow pavement, and she could only pass by stepping ostentatiously into the road.

'It was Jason Kent, wasn't it?'

The man looked so interested that time that Virginia said firmly:

'Why do you want to know all this? I'm afraid I'm not used to being questioned in this way.'

'Well, you see'—he hesitated, and then seemed to make up his mind to be frank—'I'm a reporter. And of course, anything about Jason Kent is news.'

'Is it?' Virginia was genuinely astonished. To accept the fact that any visitor of theirs was well-known was difficult enough, but that his affairs should actually be worthy of comment in a newspaper seemed fantastic.

'Well, of course. Nobody else seems to have got on to this accident yet. He's been very badly injured, hasn't he?'

'The doctor was worried about him at first. But I don't think I can really talk further about him. After all, he is a guest and—'

'That's all right, Miss—?' Virginia failed to supply the name, and the journalist ran on cheerfully at once. 'People like Jason Kent are used to being talked and written about. To be quite frank, what I heard was that he probably won't walk again, and, of course, there's a terrific story in a man like Kent suddenly being crippled.'

'How did you get hold of *that* idea?' Virginia asked coldly. She suddenly felt indignantly protective about Jason Kent again even if he had made her—very angry. She didn't want this babbling, careless young man to get hold of the tragedy that had happened and serve it up as a tasty bit of news for a million breakfast tables. But her questioner was unabashed.

'As a matter of fact, I got it from his wife.'

'His wife! Then why not ask her whatever else you want to know?' Virginia suggested with a chilliness that would have done credit to Aunt Julia.

'Oh, I don't *know* her,' was the candid reply. 'But I had a lucky break last night. She came into the restaurant where I happened to be dining. I recognised her at once. She was Ginette Darnley before her marriage, you know.'

Virginia did not know, and waited coldly for the rest of the story.

'She was with one or two friends—sat at the table next to mine—and was telling them about Kent. Even spoke of the house in a way that made it pretty easy to identify. A great piece of luck for me.'

'It must have been,' Virginia agreed dryly. 'But I'm afraid you couldn't have eavesdropped very accurately. Mr Kent is going on very well, and I think you would be unwise to report anything sensational about his illness. Good morning.'

And this time she stepped into the road and, in spite of a further effort to detain her, walked on rapidly and in at the gate.

When she got into the house Virginia judged from the indignation on Aunt Julia's face that the reporter had actually had the temerity to call there before he had spoken to her.

'A very vulgar man in a rain coat,' she told her niece.

'Yes. He asked me questions, too.'

'I hope,' said Aunt Julia, 'that you sent him about his business.'

'I wasn't very informative, Aunt Julia.'

'I am glad. Such impertinence! Coming up to the front door as bold as brass.'

Virginia wondered idly if an approach by the tradesmen's entrance would have been any better received. But for the moment she let it pass, and the regrettable reporter was allowed to join the list of painful subjects not mentioned at Aunt Julia's table.

But, all the same, he left a considerable impression on Virginia—not for himself, but for the light he shed on Jason Kent and his position in the world.

During the day there was no question of her having to go in to see Kent. The nurse had left instructions that he was to asleep. But as evening drew on, Virginia was conscious of an increasing and (as she told herself) absurd nervousness.

She would have to sit up with him to-night—that was, unless he was well enough to be left. She could not imagine that Aunt Julia would take on such a task every night.

Virginia's anticipations were quickly confirmed. As soon as tea was over, Aunt Julia said:

'Jinny, you'd better go and lie down for a while, otherwise you'll find sitting up too tiring.'

And as there was nothing to say except: 'Very well, Aunt Julia,' Virginia said it, and went to her room.

She was not sleepy. She lay on her bed, wide awake, wondering uncomfortably what Jason's reaction would be when he saw her again. Probably by now he either felt a bit of a fool. In either case he would surely prefer to make no reference to what had happened.

That, of course, would be the best solution all round. And yet she found it difficult to believe that their sarcastic, mocking visitor would really let well alone. He would almost certainly tease her a little about her annoyance, and make one or two of those half-smiling remarks that always left her wondering just exactly what he did mean.

Well, what of it? He could not stay there for ever, and when he was gone the whole experience could be dismissed as a sort of day-to-day unpleasantness which had to be endured for a while, but left no lasting impression.

He was asleep when she came in, and one glance at his pale, unconscious face made her feel that he was not so formidable after all.

He was thinner, she could not help thinking—at least his face was. Or else it was just that the shadows made it appear so. He looked as though he had gone through a bad and exhausting day or two, and as she sat down by the fire, Virginia began to wonder just why she had been so much offended—or rather, hurt—by what he had said.

After all, it was probably only a careless remark, flung off by a sick and impatient man, almost without thinking. It had been silly of her to mind so much. She supposed it was the fact that it had also touched so nearly on a desperately painful problem which had made her exaggerate the whole thing to herself. A pity, but it was over now, and if only he didn't——

'Virginia, is that you?' He spoke just then from the bed, softly and rather sleepily. She glanced over quickly.

'Yes. Did I wake you?'

'No.' There was a pause. Then: 'Why have you stayed away such a long time?'

'It wasn't so—very long,' she said evasively.

'It seemed like it.'

Virginia wondered whether she should take that as a compliment or a reproach.

'Did it? I'm sorry—' She found she was. 'But I didn't think it was necessary to come in while you were asleep, and then—well, Aunt Julia took a turn at sitting up last night.'

He offered no comment on her, but the silence was not complimentary.

After a moment he spoke again.

'Was that your only reason for staying away?'

'Well—' She paused embarrassedly. Apparently he was *not* going to let the matter rest.

'Come over here. I can't see you well.' He spoke imperiously, but a little appealingly, too.

She was not sure that she wanted him to see her well, but she could hardly refuse to come.

As she crossed the room, his dark, restless eyes were fixed on her.

'Have I offended you again?' The enquiry was abrupt, and he took her hand in his as though he thought it might scare her away.

Virginia looked down at the strong, rather thin fingers that were holding hers so tightly. She felt suddenly young and inexpereinced and, for no special reason, as though tears were not far off. In answer to his query, she only nodded.

'Very much?'

'I was very cross at the time—not so much now.'

He laughed slightly at that. Then he became serious again. 'Would you be very much surprised,' he said slowly, 'to hear that I'm quite overwhelmingly sorry?'

'*Are* you sorry?' she asked.

Very lightly and charmingly he kissed the hand he was holding, before he let it go. 'I was horribly rude and unkind to you, Virginia. Will you forgive me?'

'Of course. It doesn't matter in the least—it's forgotten. But I'm not a child, you know,' Virginia added rather irrelevantly.

'No? Eighteen, wasn't it? It seems very pleasantly young when you are my age.'

She looked at him then—perhaps with the interest she felt, showing in her face.

'A good fifteen years older than you, Virginia,' he told her amusedly, as though in answer to the look. 'And about fifty years older in general wickedness and experience, I suppose.'

'I don't think you're wicked at all,' Virginia said gravely.

'But then you don't really know much about me, do you?' He was still amused.

'Well—yes, I think I do.'

'So?' His eyebrows went up. 'What do you know about me?'

'You've been very much spoilt.'

'Hm-hm. By whom? Fate?'

'I think perhaps—by women.'

That didn't seem to embarrass him in the least. In fact, she was the embarrassed one. She turned her grave blue eyes away from him and looked at the fire, while for his part he remained perfectly cool, considering her statement.

'Yes,' he conceded thoughtfully, 'I dare say I have been rather spoilt by women. Does that shock you?'

'No. I suppose when a man is as good-looking as you, it is almost inevitable.'

He laughed.

'Well—yes, I suppose I've always got my own way a good deal more than was good for me.'

'You mean that you—that you——'

'Took my fun where I found it? Rather so, if I must confess it. Only, of course, the "fun" is pretty pointless, empty stuff when one looks back on it.'

'Which rather serves you right, doesn't it?'

'Oh, undoubtedly,' he agreed gravely. 'Judging by the standards of Aunt Julia, no doubt this accident was richly deserved retribution for a misspent youth.'

'I don't think you deserved the accident at all. And I don't expect the youth was so misspent.'

'I'm not sure that I should want *you* to know all about it.' He spoke lightly, but with a certain ring of sincerity.

Virginia didn't answer that. Just sat there, looking very grave and reflective.

'I won't be so banal as to offer a penny for your thoughts,' Jason said at last, 'but——'

She sighed quickly, as though recalled to the present from a long way off.

'I was only thinking about Richard. The situation isn't getting any better.'

'Worse?'

She nodded.

'At least, the effect on him is getting worse every day.'

She was too much occupied with her own thoughts to notice that he was watching her now with slightly narrowed eyes, and the thoughtful way his teeth pressed on his lower lip showed that he was making up his mind to something which caused him some doubts.

'Virginia——'

She looked up.

'You realise, don't you, that you and I have got into the way of speaking very frankly to each other? I've shocked you and I suppose I've upset you more than once in our short acquaintance, but still I feel that with you it's silly to wrap things up.'

'Well—yes, of course. I'd rather you said whatever it is you want to say quite frankly.' She wondered a good deal what was coming, but even after this reassurance he still chose his words rather carefully.

'I have a proposition to make to you. It isn't a very—laudable proposition, I suppose. In fact, conventional people would probably call it disgraceful.'

'I'm not very conventional,' Virginia said gravely, whereat he smiled—a little as though he disagreed. And then apparently he decided to begin at the other end of the subject.

'Would you like to earn twenty thousand pounds, Virginia?'

The colour rushed into her face and then as rapidly receded. 'Twenty thousand pounds? Are you serious? It's a fortune!'

'Oh, no!' He laughed at such an idea. 'It's nothing like a fortune, but I dare say it would be enough to do whatever you want to do for your brother and to train you for some sort of profession yourself.'

For a moment she could say nothing. The almost careless phrases opened such a vista of blinding, sunlit happiness that she was wordless and breathless. No more misery for Richard, no more anxiety when his letters came. No more tyranny from Aunt Julia. No more grey, loathly, resentful boredom, with the ever-present goad of a frantic desire to escape.

This *was* escape! Escape! ESCAPE!

'What is there in the world that could earn me twenty thousand pounds?' she asked in a hoarse, incredulous whisper. 'I'd do anything. But of course'—and suddenly the flame died down to grey, grey ashes—'of course, you didn't really mean it, did you? You were just making one of those half-joking remarks that I always take the wrong way.'

'On the contrary, I did mean it—every word.' He spoke crisply and forcefully, not at all like a sick man now.

'Listen, Virginia, we'll have all the cards on the table. I've told you how I detest my wife. Please don't waste time being shocked about it. This isn't the moment to say the things one ought to say; it's the moment to say the things one means. Our marraige is dead. I'm desperately, frantically sick of her and I'd do anything to be free of her as soon as possible. So she must divorce me. That is where you come in.'

'You're asking me to be cited in your divorce?' Virginia wondered very much how she got the words out, and then why the roof of Aunt Julia's house didn't fall in and crush her.

'Technically, yes. If you've any strictly moral qualms, you can dismiss them. I like women, but I won't take advantage of the situation.' He smiled grimly. 'But I shall want you to live there in my house.'

'Is that—absolutely—necessary?'

'Absolutely. You must do something to earn your twenty thousand, you know,' he added dryly. 'I'm sorry if you don't like it—but there it is. I must have a cast-iron case to satisfy Ginette, and it must be something that will touch her pride, too. If she thought I was only doing to to get rid of her, she would coolly hang on from spite. But if she were humiliated to the extent of having another woman brought into her own house, then—'

'It's rather a terrible idea!' Virginia's voice shook.

'Very well, it's a terrible idea, if you like to look at it that way,' he agreed impatiently, 'but at least it's a practical idea. I don't know what's specially terrible about it, as a matter of fact. There's no outrage to anyone's deep feelings. A certain amount of chagrin for Ginette, a certain amount of embarrassment for you and a certain amount of expense for me. Beyond that, the results seem to me to be definitely on the credit side.'

Virginia was silent, turning over the strange, callous

proposition in her mind. It was no good pretending even to herself that she was too shocked to consider it. She *was* considering it now—this very moment.

It was a cynical arrangement—even disgraceful, she supposed—but perhaps no more cynical than a good many marriages which passed muster as respectable.

Against the law? Well, yes, she reflected uneasily, perhaps it was that, but that part of it didn't actually appal her. And against all this, there was the thought that Richard—

'There's one thing I must point out to you.' His voice broke in coolly. 'In the eyes of your aunt—and, for all I know, other people whose opinion you value more—you'll be absolutely beyond the pale. There'll be no question of my marrying you after it's all over. I want to be *free*. Probably I shall feel I don't want to set eyes on you again—and for that matter, you'll certainly feel that way about me.'

'Why are you so sure of that?' She asked the question without being able to help it.

'Because I have it on Ginette's authority that no one could live in the same house with me for six months without detesting me,' he told her.

'It would have to be *so* long?' She looked startled.

'Oh, yes. To begin with, I can't tell how long it will be before I'm well and able to get about again.' She realised with wonder that he no longer even entertained the idea of being permanently disabled. His energetic pursuit of what he wanted seemed to him to transcend every other possibility. 'At the moment'—he laughed shortly—'I'm hardly convincing as the erring husband. The idea would have to be that we—took such a fancy to each other that we couldn't face separation. You would come with me to London—or follow me immediately—whichever was less unpleasant for you, in view of the probable reaction of your aunt. Once you were living in my house, the question of when, where—or even whether— we actually overstepped the bounds of propriety would concern no one but ourselves. Technically you would be regarded as—'

'Yes, I understand.' Virginia interrupted him rather hastily and breathlessly before he could say the word again.

He accepted the interruption, and waited, smiling a little, for what she would say.

'And it's really worth Twenty thousand pounds to you to have this done?'

'Most certainly.'

Slowly she raised her head and looked into the cool, dark eyes which regarded her so steadily.

'I accept,' she said.

CHAPTER FOUR

VIRGINIA thought the week following this conversation was the strangest and most restless she had ever spent. Not that she had any wish to go back on her decision. Her mind was made up and she allowed no misgiving to shake her determination.

But it was strange to sit opposite her aunt at meal-times and think:

'Soon I shall be gone. For better or worse, I shall be out of this terrible house. If Aunt Julia could know what I am thinking, she'd kick me out now. Well, I don't care. I don't care!'

It was strange too to go in and out of Jason Kent's room, sit up with him at night, watch him as he slept, and think:

'Soon I shall be living in his house—regarded by the world as his property, something he values and even loves. I shall live a life I've never known before, with all the values different, and everything will be subject to his will—or his whim, come to that. What do I really know about him? What sort of man is he that his own wife detests him? I don't know—I have no means of telling. He's strangely likeable, ill like this, in spite of his strange outlook and his idea that he can run the world to suit himself. But what's he like in ordinary circumstances?'

And then, when news came from Richard, she would think:

'Never mind, it isn't for long. Richard's life is really going to begin quite soon. I'll have to think up some story to tell him. I've never lied to him before, but I must now. He wouldn't hear of my doing this, but once it's done, he can't

47

object. But I'll have to pretend very hard because otherwise he might not take the money. Suppose, after all this, he wouldn't take the money! Oh, I mustn't risk that. I'll have to tell him something that will satisfy him. But it isn't going to be easy.'

It wasn't going to be easy. That was the one conclusion that emerged from all her feverish thinking. But, characteristically, she was not dismayed by it. Her only real fear was lest the whole plan should vanish into thin air—somehow prove to be nothing but a figment of an imagination fevered by anxiety and despair.

Or suppose he changed his mind? Suppose it seemed as fantastic to him now as it had to her at first? Cold perspiration broke out on her at the thought. She couldn't bear it— she *could not bear it,* if the whole plan fell through now.

And then she calmed herself. It would not fall through. Every word and look of his had spoken of determination. It would not fall through.

'I suppose I must be naturally rather an immoral person,' Virginia told herself dispassionately. 'I'm going to embark on what Aunt Julia would certainly call "a life of vice," and yet I haven't a qualm about it. At least, I think I haven't.'

And then she went upstairs to see how the cause of all this was getting on.

In the last few days they had spoken remarkably little to each other of what was so much in their thoughts. Perhaps Jason felt that all which needed saying had been said. Or perhaps he was afraid of scaring her by discussing the project. That he was the least embarrassed she could not imagine for one moment. Nor could she credit him with having any scruple of conscience.

That afternoon, when she came in, he was lying slightly propped up, and he seemed very satisfied to see her.

'Come in, Virginia. I have some news for you,' he said at once.

'Good news?'

'As you care to look at it. Doctor Brown has decided to move me next week.'

'Oh, good! Then it must mean you're getting better.'

'Don't be a hypocrite, Virginia,' he said coolly. 'You know quite well that isn't the aspect which is supposed to interest you.'

'I suppose so. When I've made a decision I don't like to wait too long before carrying it out.'

'Good girl,' he remarked approvingly.

'Do you know which day you go?'

'No. That will depend on circumstances. Towards the end of the week, I imagine. Now, do you want me to see your aunt and explain that you're coming with me?'

'*Tell* Aunt Julia? To her face? Good heavens, no!'

'Then you're not going to tell her at all?'

'No. I shall just go out of the house and—and leave a note, I suppose.'

'A little melodramatic,' he suggested.

'I can't help that. It's the most peaceful way of doing things.'

He made a slight face.

'I should have thought you would have enjoyed telling your aunt flatly that she no longer had any power over you.'

'Oh, no. I just want to get away, that's all.'

'So?' He seemed to find that a rather spineless way of doing things. 'I shall not reduce my explanations to letter-writing,' he remarked with a touch of malice. 'I'm going to enjoy telling Ginette that I am bringing another woman home, and inviting her to leave.'

'Oh! Don't you think you—we—ought to go somewhere else? I mean, it's rather awful—in her own home——'

'No. *My* home,' he corrected coldly. 'It was my home—my family home long before I brought her there. I'm fond of the place. She cares nothing about it. I—loved my home. She made me hate it. At least she'll not drive me from it.'

Virginia had never heard him speak with anything so near passion before, and it moved and disturbed her.

'I hope,' she said slowly, 'that it will never be my lot to make you very angry.'

'Why?' He laughed impatiently. 'Anyway, you're almost sure to.'

'Why? Are you so easy to anger?'

'I don't know. Yes, fairly easy, I suppose.' And then, as she didn't answer that, he glanced at her and his expression softened curiously. 'But perhaps it's not very easy to be angry with you.'

The rather wistful expression did not leave her eyes, and, after a moment, he brushed the digression aside.

'Then it's settled that you follow me a day or two after my departure. I'll let you know when it will be—convenient for you to come.'

'Very well.'

'And then you'll write your letter of explanation to Aunt Julia and slip away, eh?'

'Yes.'

'Well, you'll need money, of course.'

'Yes. I'm sorry.'

'Why? There's no need to be. Aunt Julia is the one whose conscience should be troubled on that point.'

Virginia smiled faintly, and then her eyes opened very wide at his next remark.

'In any case,' he explained carelessly, 'you'll only be anticipating your first month's allowance by a few days.'

'My—allowance?'

'Of course. Hadn't you thought of that?'

'You mean a part of the twenty thousand pounds?'

'Oh, no, Virginia.' He seemed amused. 'That's a lump sum for—well, for services rendered, I suppose. You'd better have half of that at the completion of it. But you'll need an allowance while you're living in my house. The people I move among live expensively, and Aunt Julia's taste in clothes, for instance, would hardly do.'

'I—see.'

She was very thoughtful now. It was curious, but that sentence, 'the people I move among live expensively,' had done more than anything else, to open her eyes to what she was doing.

She saw herself now—moving among them, too—noticed curiously by them—commented on as 'Jason Kent's girl-friend you know.' Oh, it was not a nice thought. Not a nice thought at all!

She looked at him.

'Shall I have to go about in public a lot with you?'

He raised his eyebrows.

'A certain amount. I'm not exactly a dazzling social light, but yes, of course, we should go about a good deal. The whole success of the idea would depend on your being noticed,' he pointed out a trifle impatiently.

'Yes, I see that.'

'Then what's the trouble?'

'There's no trouble.'

He frowned, and just for a moment Virginia had the idea he was going to call the whole thing off—declare it was a farce or a shame or something which would prevent its being carried out. She must not let that happen—she must not! There was Richard.

'It's very nice of you to give me an allowance. I hadn't thought of that, as you say. I'll try not to cost you a lot.'

'Oh, you funny child.' Jason laughed, not quite as she had heard him laugh before. Rather as though he were moved and didn't want to show it. 'Here, find me my wallet, will you? I think it's in that drawer there with all the other things from my pockets.'

She found the wallet and brought it to him.

As he took it, she noticed again how thin his fingers were. In the ordinary way, he must have very powerful hands, she thought. Now——

He peeled several bank notes off the wad that was in his case. She was so shaken at the thought of holding so much money in her hand that she couldn't even take in whether they were five- or ten-pound notes.

'I—I don't need all that,' she stammered. 'Only my fare and——'

'Oh, yes, you do,' he assured her carelessly. 'Good heavens, child! You're the only woman I ever met who hadn't a natural aptitude for spending money. There's something to be said for Aunt Julia's upbringing, after all.'

'Because I shan't cost you much?' Virginia smiled.

'No, my dear. Because there will be a certain amount of pleasure in spending money on a woman who considers one generous instead of mean.'

'I can't imagine your being mean,' Virginia said earnestly. 'Other things, perhaps—but not mean.'

'No?' He laughed. 'Ginette would not agree with you.'

Virginia thought of the mink and the pearls which had adorned his wife.

'Perhaps,' she ventured, 'she's naturally extravagant.'

'Perhaps she is, Virginia. Or perhaps it's just something all you women learn as soon as you get your hands on a rich man. In six months' time even you may be upbraiding me for meanness.'

'I don't think that's likely,' Virginia said soberly, whereat he laughed.

'No? Well, we shall see. Now, you needn't stay any longer. I think I want to sleep.'

So Virginia went, the banknotes folded into a tight little wad in the palm of her rather cold hand.

Three, four more curious days slipped by. Aunt Julia

remarked that when they did get rid of their visitor it would be time to begin the spring-cleaning.

'I shall start you on washing the china right away, Jinny. We've got very much behindhand with your doing so much night duty.'

She spoke rather as though the night duty had been a riotous indulgence of Virginia's own making. But Virginia didn't care. Let Aunt Julia talk of washing china if she liked. She—Virginia—would not be there to wash much of it.

In spite of what Aunt Julia said about 'night duty', it had not been necessary for anyone to sit up with their patient for the last few nights. But this night—his last in the house, for he was leaving the next day—Virginia woke about two o'clock—wide awake, startled and somehow anxious.

She sat up in bed and listened—she hardly knew for what. But there was no sound.

It was all right. There was nothing that need worry her. Jason would be quietly asleep.

But the anxiety persisted. He might be worse. She ought to go and see for herself. He might want something, and there was no one there to get it.

She got out of bed and pulled on her dressing-gown. She couldn't find her slippers in the dark and didn't dare put the light on for fear of disturbing her aunt, but it didn't matter because his room was just across the passage from hers.

She slipped out of her room and softly opened his door. The light had been turned out, but there was a glow from the heater in the room, and he must have seen her as soon as she came in.

'Is that you, Virginia?' he said rather drowsily. 'Come here. What is it?'

She came over to the bed.

'It—it isn't anything really. I just happened to wake up,

and I thought you might want something. A drink perhaps—'

He smiled at her.

'No, I don't want anything. Did you really get out in the cold just for that?'

'Oh, it isn't very cold really.'

'Yes, you're shivering.'

He sounded shocked at the discovery. Almost as shocked as she was that he should bother about it.

'It doesn't matter.'

'Yes, it does. Go back to bed before you catch cold.'

'And you're sure you don't want anything?'

She bent over him, smiling, and as she did so a long strand of her bright, fair hair fell over her shoulder.

'Nothing,' he said with his eyes on her hair, and, putting out his hand, he took the strand rather wonderingly. 'It's very beautiful.'

She laughed and put up her hand to draw the strand of hair away again. As her fingers touched his, she exclaimed:

'Why, how cold you are. Wouldn't you like a hot drink?'

There was a perceptible pause before he said with an effort:

'No, thanks.'

'I think you would. I'm going to get one.'

He didn't say anything to that or make any further attempt to detain her. But his eyes followed her right to the door.

Virginia stood by the stove in the cold kitchen, watching the bubbles gather round the sides of the saucepan, listening mechanically for the hiss of the boiling liquid when it rose in the pan. Her expression had not changed. To all appearances she was still intent on the small task before her. Only a slight pallor and the fact that her eyes had widened and darkened bore any witness to the fact that Virginia had suffered a blinding moment of self-revelation.

For the first time in her life she deliberately tried to escape facts. Taking the saucepan from the stove, she carefully poured the drink into a cup, as though nothing more important stirred her consciousness. But she saw with dismay that her hand was trembling.

'It's for Richard really,' she half-whispered to herself. 'Of course it's for Richard that I'm going to do it. And for myself, too. It—it means so much.'

A business deal with a cynical man—a deal that was to the advantage of both of them. That was what it was.

She thought of Jason taking hold of her hair and telling her it was beautiful. Of the way he always talked to her.

No one in all her life had cared even a little bit about what happened to her. Funny how one curious flicker of interest in her had melted her heart, and shown her more of herself than all the months as Geoffrey's fiancée had done.

But then it wasn't just the words. It was that *he* had spoken them. With a slight shiver she conceded that fact —allowed herself to draw a step nearer the truth.

'But it's such a little while. Only days really! Two weeks ago I didn't know him.' She could have cried the words aloud.

Perhaps though it didn't take more than two weeks for the whole world to change. And it had changed. With a little sigh that was hardly even protesting, she gave up the struggle. *Her* world had changed.

Two weeks ago it had centred round Richard—and the dark shadow in it had been Aunt Julia. Now it was rapidly centring round the strange, overbearing man upstairs, and the dark shadow in it was that he only needed her services for six months. Her *services*—not anything else at all.

Well, wasn't even that something? Wasn't that what she wanted?—to look after him, do things for him? There would be the strangest pleasure in that. He might be arrogant, unreasonable, even unkind quite often. But he was *alive*!

Not cheerless and petty and lifeless like her aunt. To do things for her was an affront to one's pride and affection. To do things for him——

And then suddenly she remembered the drink she was holding. If she didn't hurry it would grow cold.

Turning out the light, she went out of the kitchen. To shut out the sight of that cold, clean, staring room helped slightly to shut away the strange thoughts which had come to her there, and almost with relief she plunged boldly into the dark well of the hall and staircase.

She was slightly breathless when she arrived back in Jason's room, and that seemed to amuse him.

'Running away from bogies?' he enquired.

'No.' She flushed and laughed a little. 'You think I'm very silly, don't you?'

He shook his head. He took the drink slowly, slightly propped up on her arm, and each time she glanced down at him she thought he looked thoughtful and even puzzled.

'What is it?' she asked at last. 'What are you thinking about so hard?'

He glanced up at her, and then said slowly, 'I was trying to think if there were one single other person I know who would help me the way you've done.'

'Oh——' She was considerably taken aback. 'But it's not much. There must be several who would.'

'Must there?' He smiled and slightly shook his head. 'Do you know, Virginia, I can't think of any. And now, thank you, Virginia. That was a very nice drink. Go along to bed. I shall sleep now.'

'You're sure?'

'Quite sure.'

She laid him back and gently put the clothes round him again.

'Goodnight, then.'

'Goodnight, Virginia.'

She slipped away out of the room—to lie wide-eyed in her bed in the room opposite, and try to convince herself that the strange feelings stirring in her were half her romantic imagination.

Jason's departure next day had the elements of both drama and comedy.

Her aunt rather ceremoniously bade him farewell—coming to his room to do it. He thanked her gravely for her hospitality. She inclined her head majestically in acknowledgment of this, and no one said anything about the extreme reluctance with which that hospitality had been extended.

Then he turned his head to look at Virginia.

'Thank you, too, Virginia, for all you've done. I hope perhaps we may meet some time in London.'

'I hope so.' Virginia was as grave as he. But Aunt Julia quickly interposed with:

'My niece very seldom goes up to Town, and *never* alone.'

'Then perhaps, when she does come,' Jason suggested politely, 'I shall have the pleasure of seeing you, too.'

The idea was not developed further, and after that the ambulance attendants came and carried him downstairs to the waiting ambulance.

Just for a moment Virginia thought: 'I hate his going! Oh, I've never hated anything so much since Richard went away. Suppose something happened and I didn't see him again? I haven't even said goodbye to him properly.'

And then she told herself not to be so silly. She would be seeing him in a few days' time.

'Now,' Aunt Julia said firmly, 'now we can settle down once more to normal life.'

She had not herself, of course, deviated in the slightest during the last two weeks from the kind of life she liked to live. What she really meant was that once more she had the right to call on every minute of Virginia's time instead of only a part of it.

The incident was closed.

So Virginia settled down to a day or two of concentrated china-washing and furniture-polishing. Aunt Julia's spring cleaning was always a grim affair, beginning in late February and continuing with increasing ferocity until the middle of April.

But this year, of course, it hardly mattered. Virginia would not be there for the final crescendo. She would be in London with Jason Kent, presumably living a life of gilded vice. At least, that was what it would be, according to the standards of Aunt Julia.

His letter arrived a few days later and Virginia collected it from the box without her aunt seeing and escaped upstairs to her room to read it in peace. It bore a London postmark and the slightly unsteady writing of a sick man.

'*Dear Virginia*,' Jason had written, with a cool economy of words. '*You may come when you please. Buy a few clothes before you put in an appearance here, and don't be afraid of spending. That money was given you to spend. Yours, Jason Kent.*'

She laughed when she read it. It was impossible not to. Had any man ever urged a girl to leave home with more prosaic wording?

Then the laughter died away.

It had come at last. Here was her charter of freedom—her ticket for the unknown. She stood poised on the edge of the future. Next year, next month, even next week, where would she be, and what would her feelings be? Would she be regretting her decision—thanking heaven she had taken it? It was impossible to tell.

She could only go on and find out for herself, however bitter the discovery might be—or however sweet.

CHAPTER FIVE

WHEN Virginia had read his letter for the second time, she made her decision. She would go that night—or rather, very early in the morning.

Why wait? There was no point in that.

If she left the house between five and six, she could walk the three miles to the nearby railway junction and pick up the first train to Town. She need take hardly any luggage. She would buy everything she needed in London. Jason had said she was to spend some of those crackling notes he had given her.

For a moment she had a few misgivings lest she would be unable to choose the sort of clothes he was evidently accustomed to. But then she remembered that there are very few women who cannot find clothes to suit them when the means are unrestricted.

The last evening at home!

How strange that was. Even saying it over to oneself was strange—and it didn't seem to become any more convincing.

Perhaps it was only her imagination, but it certainly seemed that Aunt Julia was more than usually oppressive and argumentative. Perhaps it was just that she was already looking at her from a distance, already taking the detached, independent view which freedom was going to give her.

Aunt Julia said goodnight at last, and, for once with absolute sincerity, Virginia expressed the hope that she would sleep well. She didn't want any interruption to the few preparations she had left to make.

During the afternoon she had already written the note she was going to leave. No amount of re-writing would make it anything but rather silly and melodramatic, as Jason Kent had said it would be, but she had somehow contrived to get down a few satisfactory lines at last.

She had had to pretend, of course, that it was a love affair between them. Aunt Julia was the kind of woman to come storming up to London and demand police intervention if she had been told the real terms of the bargain. Virginia hoped it all sounded convincing, but actually she had trembled a little when she wrote down in black and white: 'You see, I love Jason and I'm going with him.' She had a superstitious feeling that it was unlucky to write that down—pretending to herself that it was a lie, and concealing from Aunt Julia that it was only half the truth, anyway.

As well as seeing to the writing of the note, she had packed her few personal belongings into a small case. That was all she was going to take with her, and it was safely concealed under her bed now.

She undressed for the last time in her cold bedroom which had seen her so often in moods of despair and rebellion. She must be careful not to oversleep, of course—it might even have been better not to have gone to bed at all —but if she could get a few hours of real rest, it would be a good preparation for the strange and tiring day which must lie before her.

Virginia did sleep—but only fitfully. Sometimes she lost consciousness for what seemed long periods, only to wake with a frantic start and grope for the clock, feeling certain that this time she had overslept. But then she would realise once more that only ten minutes had passed, and sink back, while the beating of her heart subsided to normal again.

Once the clock showed half-past four, however, she dared not go to sleep again. Creeping out of bed, shivering with cold, she began to drag on her clothes.

This didn't seem much like a dramatic elopement, or even a courageous bid for freedom. Least of all did she feel like a bold venturer on the path of vice. She only felt cold and depressed and slightly sick, and her chief longing was for a hot bath

However, it was no good thinking of those things now.

She was ready—but even now, much too early. She thought at first that she would slip away at once. It would be better to wait at the railway station—where at least she could probably have a hot wash in the waiting-room—than linger here on the edge of indecision.

Then she reflected that if by some chance her absence were discovered soon after she had gone, there would still be time to follow her (and Aunt Julia would, too!) and some dreadful attempt would be made to bring her back.

So she sat by the window instead, watching the grey light grow stronger, picking out the familiar outlines of the garden she would know no more.

Her head drooped wearily, and she leant it against the side of the window-frame. She must not sleep, but at least she could close her eyes for a moment. It might be a good idea to start thinking out how she was going to act when she arrived in London.

It would still be comparatively early in the morning—early enough to make breakfast and a wash and brush-up the first essentials. She was a little vague about where to breakfast, because she had very seldom been to London, and then only with Aunt Julia in close attendance. But she would find some place.

Then she would have to go shopping—not, she supposed, at the long-established, homely shops loftily patronised by Aunt Julia, but in those bright, glittering places past which she had always been hurried, while Aunt Julia muttered, 'Trash' or 'Positively indecent'.

Finally, she would have to effect the miraculous change from a chrysalis to a slightly wicked butterfly—and for that she would need some sort of room of her own.

An hotel? Did one take a room at an hotel for an hour or two in the middle of the day? It seemed rather unusual. Yet Jason Kent evidently expected her to arrive in her transformed state.

It was at that point that she remembered Jessica Young the casual, sophisticated, but oddly likeable fashion artist who had stayed with Dr Brown's family last summer. She had taken something of a fancy to Virginia at the time and made her promise that if ever she came to London she would look her up. Virginia had never imagined she would have any occasion to do so, but now the invitation might prove very useful. Anyway, she would see.

With another of those starts, she realised that consciousness had been slipping away again. She glanced once more at the clock, and this time it was really time to go.

A horrid, nerve-racking moment. But perhaps not quite so nerve-racking now that she had remembered Jessica Young.

Very softly Virginia opened her door.

Not a sound. The upstairs landing stretched, dim and silent, in front of her. Quietly she crept along it, and began the perilous descent of the stairs. By keeping close to the wall stepping over the third and eighth stairs, she accomplished the journey without any of those pistol-shot sounds which creaking stairs give forth in a silent house.

She slipped across the hall and into the kitchen. The front door was too dangerously noisy a proposition to attempt, and quite impossible to close silently after her. Carefully she drew back the two bolts and turned the two keys which Aunt Julia considered necessary to guard the back door.

Cyrus, the great Persian cat, roused himself from his basket and gazed at her with bright, supercilious eyes. He despised her for what she was doing, obviously, but then he despised nearly everybody. Perhaps eight years in Aunt

Julia's house had given him a poor opinion of human nature.

'Goodbye, Cyrus,' Virginia whispered, and slipped out, closing the door quietly after her.

Her footsteps sounded appallingly loud to her on the gravel of the garden path, but perhaps that was only imagination, because her heartbeats sounded even louder.

Only the garden gate to negotiate now—it creaked very slightly, but not enough to matter—and then she was free.

She ran at first, from sheer relief and lightness of spirits, and also just to put as much distance as possible between her and the hated house. Then she dropped into a steady walk.

Out in the open air she even felt less afraid of acknowledging her own feelings.

She was going to him! Today she was going to see him. Life was beginning again.

Once she had trembled because six months was the limit of the time that stretched before her. Six months? A lifetime. An eternity. What could one not make of six months if the gods were kind?

She arrived at the station ten minutes before the train came in, but no one was there to observe her. No one, that was, except the sleepy clerk who reluctantly opened the ticket office in order to sell her a ticket.

'Return?' he enquired with a prodigious yawn.

'No,' Virginia said, and under her breath she added: 'Never!'

It was an uneventful journey, and by a quarter to nine she was already at Waterloo.

The noise and the hurrying City crowds confused her a little, but they also brought the comforting feeling that among these millions one could be safely lost. No long arm of Aunt Julia could reach her there.

She decided in the end to look up Jessica Young before breakfasting. If she delayed too long, she might miss her.

So, making her way to the long line of telephone boxes, Virginia put through a call to the Hampstead number which Jessica had given her last summer.

During the few seconds she had to wait for the connection, Virginia became agitatedly sure that Jessica was away. She was so busy, so much in demand. It was absurd to suppose she would be free just this day, of all days. She was beginning to wonder in panic what fresh course she could take, when a clear, self-confident voice said:

'Jessica Young speaking.'

'Oh, Jessica, I'm so glad! This is Virginia. Do you remember?—Virginia Baron——'

'Why, of course! Where are you speaking from? Not the country, surely?'

'No, no, from Waterloo Station. I've just arrived and I want to see you—very badly. If you could manage it, that is.' Virginia was used to having her wishes immediately countered.

'I'd be delighted. Have you had your breakfast yet?'

'No, but——'

'Thank heaven someone keeps the same civilised hours that I do! Most of my friends get active about eight o'clock —I don't know why. But anyway, you get in a taxi right away and come along. I'll have the breakfast ready by the time you arrive.'

'Oh, thank you! I'll come straight there.'

Virginia felt herself smiling in a way she never smiled at home. It was not just that Jessica was in—nor even that she was very hungry and the suggestion of breakfast was welcome. It was—oh, the beauty of being able to do what one wanted—make careless, easy plans, without someone saying 'Don't' just for the lovely sound of the word.

She rang off, and came out of the telephone box into the station once more, feeling a different being from the anxious girl who had gone in.

After that, it seemed fairly simple to be hailing a taxi for the first time in her life.

Jessica was as good as her word. When Virginia arrived at the flat, it was to find her hostess, arrayed in a startling but becoming housecoat, just bringing to the table a good supply of bacon and eggs and a pot of superb-smelling coffee.

Her greeting was casual on the surface, but kindly, and the rather haphazard arrangement of the meal secretly soothed Virginia, whose life had been overfull of restrictions.

'We'll eat first and talk afterwards, shall we?' Jessica suggested. 'I have the morning free—and most of the afternoon, too, come to that. So unless your time is short, we can idle pleasantly. What's the good of having spare time if you can't enjoy yourself wasting it?'

Wondering very much what Aunt Julia would have said to that theory, Virginia laughed and assured Jessica that she was in no hurry.

'You're stopping in London overnight, then?'

There was a slight pause.

'I'm not—going back at all,' said Virginia. 'But that's the whole story.'

'I see.' Jessica's strongly marked eyebrows rose rather steeply, but she forbore to ask any more questions until breakfast was disposed of, the dishes piled in the sink to be washed later, and the two of them seated comfortably in front of the fire in her studio.

'So you've more or less run away from home?' Jessica thoughtfully lit a cigarette. 'Well, I'm not surprised. The only puzzle to me is that you didn't do it before.'

'There wasn't much opportunity.'

'And now the opportunity has come?' Jessica looked interested.

'Yes. I believe the usual way of putting it is—I've thrown my cap over the windmill.'

Jessica laughed, and her eyebrows went up again.

'That usually implies a man in it, too,' she said lightly.

There was a long silence. Then, in quite a different tone, she went on:

'Is *that* what's happened, Virginia?'

'Yes.'

Jessica paid that the tribute of a long whistle.

'I thought you were engaged. Geoffrey Someone-or-other, wasn't it?'

'That's broken off?'

'And this is the sort of—reflex action?'

'Oh, no. I wasn't really in love with Geoffrey.'

'And with this man you are?'

Funny that she had to come to that part of it right away.

'Yes,' Virginia said deliberately, 'I am.'

There was another short pause, as though Jessica hardly knew what question to ask next.

'I take it he's a London man?' she said at last.

'Oh, yes. That's why I'm here.' Then Virginia took the plunge. 'Have you heard of Jason Kent?'

'Yes, of course. I heard from the Browns about his being smashed up outside your house. Has that got something to do with this business?'

Virginia nodded.

Jessica waited, still not jumping to what Virginia considered the very obvious conclusion.

'Well, he's the man.'

'*He* is? Jason Kent!' Jessica actually got to her feet in her astonishment. She was dismayed, too, Virginia could see. 'You can't be serious. There's some mistake.'

'Oh no. Why should there be?'

Jessica sat down slowly again, her face exceedingly troubled.

'Why, Virginia, you can't even know him very well.'

Virginia considered that. *Did* she know him very well?

She rather thought she knew him better than most people, but it was difficult to explain that to anyone as literal-minded as Jessica.

'I nursed him all the while he was in the house,' she said at last.

'But you didn't know him before that at all?'

'Oh, no.'

'My dear, of course it's your own business entirely, but——'

'But what, Jessica?'

'Well'—Jessica moved uncomfortably—'he's an incredible sort of person for you to get yourself mixed up with. Sophisticated, rather disillusioned, I should imagine, and very much a man of the world. I don't mean any disparagement to you, Virginia, when I say I can't imagine his being genuinely keen on you for a moment.'

Virginia dug her nails into the palms of her hands. She had not expected the conversation to be quite so difficult as this. It would have been so much simpler to have told Jessica the real truth, of course—but then, she and Jason had got to start *somewhere* with the story they were going to tell the world. It was no good telling some people one thing and some another.

'You mean that, frankly, you don't know what he sees in me?' she suggested very calmly.

'No, I don't mean that at all. At least, I can quite imagine what lots of men would see in you. I think you're a very attractive girl in your own quite individual way. But I can't believe it's the kind of attraction that would appeal to anyone like Jason Kent.'

'Do you know him very well, Jessica?'

'No, I don't *know* him in the real sense at all. I met him only once, and then just casually.'

'Then how can you tell?'

'Well,' Jessica gave a worried laugh. 'Just the way any experienced person who goes about a good deal would tell, I suppose. It's fairly common knowledge.'

'What is?' Virginia sounded obstinate.

'What I said—the type of man he is. Very attractive, no doubt—very good-looking, in a blasé, not-so-young-as-he-was way, but—— Oh, one would need a certain technique to manage him, Virginia, a certain—hardness to protect oneself against his particular type of cynicism and callousness. You simply haven't got it. It's like expecting a child to swim a whirlpool.'

'Don't you think you're exaggerating?' Virginia flushed angrily. 'I'm *not* a child, and—and he does love me.' She wanted to cry suddenly when she had said that, but instead she managed to look determined and slightly offended.

'I didn't say you were a child.' Jessica was quite patient about it and very much in earnest. 'And I admit from the start that it isn't really my business. But since you *have* come here to spill the beans to me, I'm going to say what I really think. Of course, I know you don't want advice. One never does, however much one may ask for it. But at least before you take this step you shall see the thing as it appears to an onlooker.'

'Very well.' Virginia smiled faintly at the determination of that. 'How does it appear to you?'

'Just as it would to any other practical person with no flies on them, I imagine. You've known this man something like a fortnight—with him ill all the time, at that. However much natural gumption you may have—and I'm not disputing that—you have practically no worldly experience, while he has the reputation of being a particularly hard nut to crack, with all the worldly experience one could ask for and then some. If he's told you he loves you, he almost certainly wants to get something out of you. Men like that don't go around dropping romantic bricks with no ulterior motive. And anyway, where does his wife come in? He's got one, hasn't he?'

'Yes. He's letting her divorce him.'

'Because of you?'

Virginia nodded.

Jessica made a face.

'You realise there'd be bound to be a good bit of mud-slinging?'

'I can't help that. Yes, I've thought of it.'

'And you think he's worth all the unpleasantness?'

'Yes.' That was very firm, perhaps because it was the simple truth.

There was a short silence.

'Are you shocked?' Virginia sounded faintly wistful.

'Well—no. At least, I'm not shocked on strictly moral grounds, if that's what you mean. I don't approve of going off and living with someone else's husband, because, apart from anything else, it usually just doesn't pay to put oneself in a false position. No doubt there *are* cases where circumstances justify it, but I don't happen to think this is one of them, that's all. To put it on its lowest level, I think you stand to lose a lot more than you're ever likely to gain.'

Virginia smiled faintly at this determinedly impersonal way of putting it.

'Well, thank you, Jessica. At least you've been perfectly frank.'

'But it does nothing to alter your decision?'

'I'm afraid not.'

'All right.' Jessica shrugged. 'I've said my say, the rest is your own affair. Sorry if I seemed interfering. I meant it for the best. But in the end one must decide these things for oneself, of course.'

'I don't think you were in the least interfering. I think it's kind of you to bother about me so much,' Virginia said earnestly. 'It won't make any difference? I mean, you don't feel you ought to stop knowing me, or anything like that?'

'Good heavens, no.'

'I'm glad.' Virginia sat looking into the fire, relieved that some sort of explanation was over. Presently Jessica spoke again.

'Was that all you wanted? Advice about something on which you'd already made up your mind?' And she smiled rather quizzically.

'Oh, no.' Virginia looked up and smiled too. 'There's something else, much more concrete, to worry about. I must get some decent clothes.'

'Yes.' Jessica ran a thoughtful eye over Aunt Julia's choice. 'Yes, I think you must, if you're going to hold your own in Jason Kent's crowd.'

'I have plenty of money.'

'Have you?'

Virginia nodded, and Jessica forbore to make any enquiries about where it came from.

'And you want to buy everything this morning?'

'Yes, if possible.'

'Meeting him this afternoon?'

'Well, I'm—going to the house. He's still ill in bed, you understand.'

'Oh, yes, of course.' Again a puzzled expression crossed Jessica's face. But almost immediately she seized, with practical energy, on the immediate problem. 'Well, my dear, it's time we started. We've got plenty to do if we're going to clothe you afresh from the skin upwards. Have you any luggage at all?'

'Nothing. Oh—except this little case with the smallest personal things in.'

'Good heavens! What a happy state!'

'To have no luggage?'

'No. To start with no left-overs and a substantial cheque —or is it notes?'

'Notes,' said Virginia. To which Jessica added:

'Yes, of course, it would be.'

Virginia never forgot that morning. All other shopping was as nothing compared to that first thrilling, almost sinful venture into the world of smart clothes—clothes such as she had never dreamed of while Aunt Julia ruled her wardrobe.

Jessica was amused at her excitement and bewilderment.

'Haven't you ever had anything decent before?' she asked with candid curiosity.

Virginia shook her head.

'Aunt Julia chose everything,' she explained simply.

'I see.' Jessica's shrewd brown eyes flickered over her. 'I think I begin to understand this cap and windmill business,' she said. But she seemed singularly dissatisfied with the increased understanding.

On their way home Jessica stopped at a hairdresser's near her flat.

'You won't find his name in the pages of *Vogue*, but he's a wizard with hair.'

'But I——'

'Now, for heaven's sake, don't start telling me you washed your hair yesterday. There are other things to do with hair besides keeping it clean.'

'I don't want it cut off.' Virginia's tone was almost sulky. She was thinking passionately, 'He *likes* my hair. Oh, that at least he does like!'

'No, of course not.' Jessica was soothing. 'But if you're going to keep on half a yard of even gorgeous hair you must learn how to do it.'

Virginia submitted, but not with a very good grace.

Only when she was seated in front of the mirror and began to see what the unusually silent little Frenchman was doing with her hair did a smile of incredulous pleasure curve her mouth.

'It's lovely hair, isn't it?' Jessica stood by, eagle-eyed, as though she were personally responsible for the masses of bright, fair hair which slid in cool strands through the Frenchman's fingers.

'*Magnifique*.'

'Don't do anything complicated with it. It must be something she can manage for herself in future.'

'It does not need anything complicated; such extravagant hair. Only that she must not draw it back so tightly. The wave must fall of its own accord here across the forehead, and again behind the ears. You understand, madame?'

He stood back finally to survey the finished dressing, and remarked:

'It will do.'

Virginia gave a quick, half-shy glance at herself in the mirror. She too thought it would do. And, having paid the quite modest bill, she collected her parcels and followed Jessica out of the shop.

At home once more in the flat, she changed into the things they had bought. Cool silk underclothes, hose that were sinfully fine and sinfully expensive, a beautiful smoke-blue suit in the latest style, the perfectly simple blouse of lighter smoke-blue which turned back to show the strong, white column of her throat—they all were utterly strange in character to Virginia, and they all helped to give her the odd sensation that she was not herself at all.

Jessica, sitting on the bed and watching her, nodded approval. 'In your odd way, you're a very beautiful girl, you know. Perhaps,' she added slowly, '*that's* what Jason Kent fell in love with.'

'Perhaps,' murmured Virginia, and hastily turned away, because it hurt badly to remember that Jason Kent had not really fallen in love with anything about her.

They went into the studio then to have tea, and just as Jessica began to pour the water into the tea-pot, a long and cheerful 'Ri-i-ing' sounded at the front door.

'Bother! We don't really want anyone, do we? Shall I take no notice?' Jessica suggested callously.

'Oh, you can't very well do that,' Virginia protested.

'Can't I! I have exactly that sort of blank conscience where my own pleasure is concerned, as a matter of fact. But anyway, it sounds like someone who'd just go on ringing. I suppose it's Clive.' And without waiting to explain who 'Clive' might be, she went to open the door.

Virginia supposed from the casual, 'Oh, it *is* you, is it?' that Clive it was, and the next moment Jessica came back into the room, followed by a tall, rather good-looking man, who was obviously very much at home there.

'My cousin Clive Graham,' she explained briefly. 'Virginia Baron—friend of mine—just arrived in London today.'

He said hello and was about to take the chair next to Virginia when Jessica observed:

'If you're scrounging tea, you'd better go and fetch your own cup and saucer.'

'I'm not scrounging. But if one *is* going to call on a dearly-loved relation, it might as well be at tea-time.' And he lounged off into the kitchen.

'He's more like a brother than a cousin really. We were brought up together,' Jessica explained. 'He has a place quite near here and drops in whenever he likes. Writes thrillers for a living, but——'

'You miserable little gossip-pedlar,' observed her cousin, coming back into the room. 'Why don't you wait until I'm right out of earshot before you talk about me? And anyway, how often have I to tell you not to disclose my guilty secret?'

Jessica grinned unrepentantly.

'He's ashamed of his thrillers,' she told Virginia.

'Oh, but why? It's very clever to be able to write them.'

'Oh, no it isn't.' Clive shook his head gloomily. 'They're

very popular thrillers. You should hear what the more superior critics say about them. I take it a critic could knock them off with his left hand, if he were not too busy criticising.'

'Well, they make money, anyway,' Jessica pointed out soothingly.

'Only aggravates the offence,' declared her cousin, reaching for a scone. 'What's money, anyway?'

Virginia thought what a lot it could be, and supposed that only people who had always had plenty talked like that. Jessica's cousin certainly had that indefinable air of money about him. It was not only the well-tailored suit or the obviously expensive gold watch on his wrist. It was the unquestioning appearance of expecting everything to go smoothly which you only find in those who have never had to know to a penny what they have in their purse.

Virginia was fascinated by the light, careless way these two seemed to take life. They expected all the right things to happen—and the strange thing was that they evidently nearly always did. Even quite serious things they spoke of with a casual, confident air that was indescribably strange after the heavy distinctions drawn by Aunt Julia.

She took very little part in the conversation herself, in spite of Clive's efforts to draw her into it. She preferred to lie back in her chair and watch the cousins, pretending to herself that this lovely, safe little interlude was lasting for ever, and that she was not rushing on towards a tremendous crisis with every minute that passed.

She noticed what pleasant grey eyes Clive had, and how very firm and decided his mouth and chin were. He might joke and laugh with Jessica, but she thought he would probably be a dependable friend in an emergency, and perhaps could be a bad enemy. His thick hair was exactly the same dark chestnut colour as Jessica's, but where hers was completely straight, his had an uneven little wave.

Oh, they were nice, thought Virginia. Nice and sane and—safe. Just for a moment she had a wild desire to stay there for ever, to find the paths of her life running in this pleasant, undemanding channel, where one never had to make momentous decisions, take indescribable risks and face a terrifying unknown.

The next moment the idea was gone, because she reminded herself that in such a life there could be no place for Jason Kent and so, quite simply, it became an impossible life for her.

It was that which stirred her to action at last.

'Jessica, if you don't mind, I think I ought to go now.'

'Well, if you'd rather.' Nothing in Jessica's tone betrayed that she knew the extremely strange errand on which Virginia was going.

Clive sat up.

'Can I give you a lift anywhere? The car's outside and I've got a free hour, if I can be of any assistance.'

It was perfectly obvious that he asked nothing better than to play escort to this new friend of Jessica's. But Virginia was appalled. The idea of arriving at Jason's house in company with another man!

'Oh, no, thank you,' she assured him hastily. 'Please don't bother.'

'It wouldn't be the slightest bother. I'd like to.'

'That's all right, Clive.' The resourceful Jessica stepped in. 'Virginia prefers to go on her own. She's—well, she's going to a new job, and she wants time to sort out her thoughts on the way. She can do that much better alone in a taxi.'

'Well—if it's like that.' He gave in reluctantly. 'What sort of a job is it? A secretaryship?'

'Something of the sort.' Again Jessica answered for her. 'Jason Kent's the employer.'

'Really? I couldn't imagine somehow— Isn't it rather brave of you to take him on?'

'Oh, no.' Somehow Virginia managed to say the words quite calmly.

'You know him personally already?'

'Yes, quite well.'

'And you—well, you like him?'

'Oh, yes.'

'You surprise me. He must have hidden depths unplumbed by the casual observer, I suppose. I always understood he was a very difficult man.'

'To work for, you mean?'

'To have anything much to do with. Let's see, didn't he have a bad motor accident quite recently?'

'Yes. That was how Virginia met him.' Once more it was Jessica who took up the explanation. 'He was brought into the house where she was living then. She helped to nurse him.'

'Caught him in a chastened mood, eh? Well, good luck. Remember me if he gives you any red-hot tips from the Stock Exchange. And if he ever lets his employees have anything so frivolous as time off, you must come out with me one evening and have dinner.'

Virginia thanked him and said she would. But she could not help wondering how much this young man's pleasant, friendly air would have changed if he could have known just what her 'job' with Jason Kent was.

In the diminutive hall of the flat she bade Jessica goodbye, trying unsuccessfully to express her thanks.

'That's all right, my dear.' Jessica brushed the thanks aside. 'Only remember one thing. If things *don't* turn out at all as you hope, or if the situation does get beyond you, don't be afraid to come here to me. I won't say "I told you so" and I'll see you don't have to go back to your aunt.'

Virginia held her hand very tightly for a moment in unspoken gratitude. Then she went out alone to the waiting taxi.

CHAPTER SIX

IT was cold in the taxi. Or else perhaps it was just the the chill of nervous anticipation had settled upon her.

But that lasted only a few minutes. Virginia found then that she was burning hot. Nerves again, she told herself. Yet she had an odd, pleasant feeling that the warmth came from her heart. She was going to see him. However much she might dread a strange future, that could not be altered. She was going to see him.

She stared out of the window at unfamiliar landmarks. There was a park on the right. A very big park, but she could not have said which one it was.

The taxi had turned out of the busier streets now, and Virginia had no idea where she was. A big, imposing, rather sombre square, with a railed-in garden in the middle. Was this where his home was—where *her* home was to be in future?

It seemed so. The taxi was stopping.

'Number 82, madame.'

The taximan this morning had called her 'miss'. She supposed the change was a tribute to her new clothes.

'Thank you.' She got out of the taxi, with her knees feeling strangely weak, and paid the fare. The man carried her new case up the steps for her and rang the big bell.

Then he returned to his cab, and drove away.

It was absurd, but at that moment even he seemed a blessedly familiar figure to Virginia, as though he were the last link with everything she knew.

But he was gone now. And she was alone.

Almost silently the big door was swinging open, and a manservant stood aside for her to enter.

She hardly took in anything of the quiet, rich, spacious hall in that first moment, and was only conscious of the odd difficulty of explaining her presence.

'I think I'm expected. Miss Baron is the name.' The words didn't come easily, but at least they *came*. The tone sounded cool and self-possessed to her own strained ears.

'Yes, madam.'

It was impossible to say whether he was agreeing that she was expected or merely commenting politely on her assertion. But he took her case from her hand and summoned a quiet, discreet-looking maid from the shadows at the back of the hall.

'Miss Baron. You will take her upstairs to her room,' he said in a low voice.

Then she *was* expected.

The girl took her up a wide, thickly carpeted staircase, where no footstep sounded. Several doors were grouped round the great square landing, and, opening one of these, she ushered Virginia into the most beautiful bedroom she had ever seen.

There were pastel grey walls and a deep-piled carpet of dusky rose covered the whole of the floor. Gleaming fitted wardrobes and cupboards were all around.

It was all Virginia could do not to exclaim aloud with pleasure and surprise.

The maid went over to the windows and quietly drew the great rose curtains, shutting out the February dusk and the last vestige of the world of reality.

'The bathroom is through here, madam.' She opened the door into a rose and silver bathroom.

'Thank you. And the other door?'

Perhaps the girl didn't hear that. At any rate, she made no answer. She just said:

'Would you like to rest a little, madam? Or will you go straight away to see Mr Kent?'

'I don't want to rest, thank you. I'll go to see him as soon as I've taken off my coat.'

'Shall I announce you?'

'No, just tell me which room it is.'

'The next one on the right here.'

Virginia realised then where that other door led, and the discovery gave her a strange sensation.

The girl withdrew, her expression quite incurious and unperturbed still. She must be well-trained, Virginia thought absently.

Slowly she took off her coat, and ran a comb through the deep, bright waves of her hair.

So that was the door into his bedroom. Strange that a few feet of passage could make all that difference. Her bedroom at home had faced his—but across a passage. Now there was no passage—only a door between.

Well, she was ready. No need to wait any longer.

She went slowly towards the communicating door. And then, on an impulse she could never afterwards explain, she went out of her room into the hall instead and knocked on the door of the next room.

'Come in.' His voice sounded cool and indifferent, as it always had.

She went in.

His room, too, was beautifully furnished, but with an indefinably masculine air about it, which, of course, she had never seen in a bedroom before.

Not that she noticed much about the room that first time. She only saw the man on the bed—the hollow dark eyes that regarded her boredly in the first moment, and then with surprise and very real pleasure.

'Virginia! Why, come here. You could only have got my letter yesterday. You must have come right away.'

'Of course.' She came over to him. 'Didn't you expect me?'

'Not really.' He took both her hands and drew her down on to the side of the bed.

'But everything was ready. There was even a room waiting for me.'

'Was there?' His smiling eyes never left her face. 'What have you done to yourself? You're different.'

'Am—am I?'

'Yes. You've done your hair differently.'

She laughed rather shyly.

'Do you like it?'

'Yes. It's lovely. I like the clothes, too.'

It was so strange—so delicious—to be approved, to have an appearance in which anyone took the slightest interest.

'I didn't choose them entirely myself. A friend came with me. She took me to the hairdresser too.'

'So?' He was not at all interested in how the result had been achieved, she saw.

Virginia looked at him more critically then. She thought he certainly looked no better than when she had last seen him—rather worse, in fact.

'What have you done to *yourself*?' she asked gently. 'You don't look so well.'

'Oh,' an impatient expression darkened his face at once, 'the journey was a bit of a trial, and I haven't been sleeping well. I suppose the scene with Ginette didn't exactly improve matters either,' he admitted with sudden candour.

'That bit serves you right.'

He frowned at her, but she saw that, as usual, her criticism was not without an amusing novelty for him.

'It wasn't a necessary scene at all. You only staged it to gratify the malicious streak in your nature.' It was fun to sit there and scold him when all the while she wanted to take him in her arms.

'You little bitch,' he retorted lazily. 'You mean you want to justify your own cowardly getaway with its melodramatic note to your detestable aunt. What did you do? Creep away in the early dawn?'

'More or less.'

'And now, I suppose, she's busy thinking that I seduced you, and will try to have my blood for decoying away an innocent girl?'

'Oh, no, I explained—in the letter.'

'What did you explain?' he asked with some curiosity.

'I told her——' Virginia stopped, hesitated, and looked suddenly confused, the more so because she knew he was amusedly watching her. 'Well, of course, I had to make some sort of pretence—say we'd fallen in love with each other, that I was going away with you—to join you, I mean. After all, we have to start the story *some* time, haven't we?'

'Of course we have.' His amusement deepened. 'I should like to have seen that note. I'm sure it did your romantic invention much credit.'

'Oh, no. It was rather feeble and stilted, really.'

'Not written in the full flood of genuine ardour? Well, that was hardly to be expected. I dare say it wasn't an easy note to write.'

'No, it wasn't.'

'At least it was a beginning, as you say. No doubt we shall both need a certain amount of practice in this business of convincing the world that we're willing to sacrifice morals, principles and even appearances to our devotion to each other. What are you going to call me, by the way?'

'How do you mean?' She was half bewildered by his quick change from banter to crude reality.

'You can hardly go on calling me Mr Kent—though, to tell the truth, I can't recall your ever having addressed me as anything.'

'I'll call you Jason, then.'

She studied him without appearing to do so, noting with a loving fear she had never experienced about anyone else but Richard, that he was terribly thin, that there were slight lines of weariness round his mouth, and that his eyes looked large and sleepless.

'Have you been trying to do things you shouldn't, since I've been away—since you came home, I mean?'

'What sort of things?' Jason spoke lazily again, but with an undercurrent of obstinacy in his tone that aroused her suspicions at once.

'You haven't been so absurd as to get in touch with your office, have you?' She was surprised to find how severe she could sound.

He turned his face away from her gaze, so that his head was almost against her arm.

'Oh, don't nag, Virginia,' he said with unexpected sulkiness.

She wanted to laugh. She terribly wanted to catch him up in her arms and laugh. To imagine this was the difficult, autocratic creature everyone said she was brave to tackle!

Very gently she drew her arm away and put it round him, lifting him carefully so that he was supported against her.

'Oh, God, that's nice.' He slumped wearily against her, his face half hidden. 'You're wonderful, Virginia.'

She didn't answer that. She was thinking with stark simplicity:

'How I love him! Oh, how I love him!'

After a while she bent her bright head and said softly:

'I suppose you *have* been working?—or trying to work?'

He frowned again and slightly pressed his cheek against her as though in protest.

'I had to. There were some things I couldn't leave. I had my secretary along here for an hour or two.'

'Without the doctor knowing, of course?'

'Well—'

'I see.' There was a pause. 'What does your own doctor say about you, now he has seen you?'

'I haven't got "my own doctor". I told you—I was never ill before in my life. The fellow Brown recommended looks very solemn and wags his head, of course—the way they all do. He brought another specialist along on Monday—Sir James Trevor. He seems to think he can do something—has a great opinion of himself. The treatment's hellish, but I suppose it's worth it if it succeeds.'

Virginia very lightly touched the dark, rebellious head that lay so close against her.

'You've had a bad day or two, haven't you?'

'Yes. It doesn't matter now, though.'

Virginia didn't ask quite what he meant by that, and he didn't offer to explain. There was a long silence, and then, when she looked down at him again, she saw he was quietly sleeping.

He had said he could not sleep at night—but he slept here in her arms very easily.

He was still sleeping there when the same maid who had shown her to her room came to ask if she would come downstairs to dinner.

'I'll come in a few minutes,' Virginia promised in a whisper, and the girl went away again.

Very gently Virginia laid him back against the pillow. He murmured protestingly, but she put her hand softly on him, and he was still again at once. She went quietly out of the room and down the stairs, wondering very much what the other people in this silent house were thinking.

There must be several servants here, obviously, and it was hardly likely that this extraordinary affair passed without comment among them.

Well, of course, she and—Jason didn't want it to pass without comment. Causing gossip was part of their plan of campaign, she supposed grimly. In that case, what the maid had just seen must have helped materially. She didn't imagine that any other woman had ever been seen sitting on the side of Jason Kent's bed, holding him in her arms.

The dining-room was as rich—and as silent—as all the other rooms in the house. The only lighting was from wall brackets and from the fire that blazed on the hearth.

It was extraordinary to sit at the head of a table instead of at Aunt Julia's left hand, and the deference with which she was waited on gave her once more the feeling that she was acting in some strange play, and that presently she would forget her part and the whole thing would end in disaster.

But the meal went off perfectly smoothly, right down to the murmured, 'Will you have your coffee in the sitting room, madam?'

'Yes, please.' She thought she would be rather more at ease there than sitting here alone at the great polished table.

The servant showed her the way across the hall to the lounge.

There was no more indication in his manner than in the maid's that he knew her position in the house. Mrs Kent herself could not have had more respectful service, and something in that helped to steady Virginia.

She had always vaguely imagined that women who did what she was supposed to be doing forfeited any outward form of respect. No doubt, even if the servants here thought their own thoughts, they were paid well to keep them to themselves, but it was soothing to find they did it so well.

The coffee was brought to her and set on a low table beside the fire. A little depressing to have to pour out only one cup, of course—and then she fell to wondering what it would be like when he was well again and they shared their meals and their leisure together.

Would she bore him unspeakably, as Jessica evidently imagined she would? Or did the odd attraction which she apparently had for him arise from something other than the fact that he was dependent on her when he was ill?

She sat forward in her chair, her hands loosely clasped, her eyes thoughtfully on the flames that licked round the huge log on the hearth.

What was her aunt doing now? she wondered idly. How had she reacted to what Jason called her 'melodramatic note'?

She found that these questions only ruffled the merest surface of her mind, as though Aunt Julia was a figure in a film which had not interested her much. It seemed incredible that one could live all one's life beside certain people, and yet feel the most perfect detachment, once one got away.

The heart-searchings of her aunt (if, indeed, she had any heart to search) interested her far less than the lightest want of the man upstairs.

But then there was Richard, too, of course. He did matter. Mattered very much indeed. She had to do something about getting in touch with him at once.

Her first impulse was to telephone. Then she remembered that he lived in digs and she wasn't sure of the number, and anyway, explanations by phone were apt to be difficult.

But she must reach him before Aunt Julia could write. Not that Aunt Julia ever did write to him, but she might on this momentous occasion. Or, at any rate, she might eventually.

'I'd better write to him myself this evening,' Virginia thought, and was indefinably relieved to find there was something she could do. To have had her every action prompted, supervised and checked all her life made it rather disturbingly novel to be left absolutely to her own devices.

She went upstairs to fetch her writing-case, lingering a few minutes to admire afresh the beautiful room which was—quite incredibly—now her bedroom.

On her way downstairs again she slipped into his room to see if he were still asleep.

She was a little startled to find a nurse there, sitting by the fire knitting. She got up at once when Virginia came in, and she, too, seemed to accept her presence without question. Jason must have given *some* sort of explanation to all these people, she supposed, and she wondered with some curiosity how he had put it.

'Good evening. He's still asleep.' The nurse spoke in little more than a whisper, and Virginia glanced over to the bed, where he lay exactly as she had left him.

'I'm glad. He hasn't been sleeping well, has he?'

'No—very badly. That's half the trouble. But I understand he has never been a good sleeper. I suppose these very clever men forget how to let their brains rest.'

'I dare say. And he's been seeing his secretary about work, hasn't he?'

'Yes.' The nurse set her mouth and shook her head disapprovingly. '*And* telephoning his office. I hope you'll be able to persuade him not to do so in future.'

Virginia was silent, really savouring the strange sensation of having it implied that, of course, she had a great deal of influence with him.

'Is he any better in himself?' she asked after a moment. 'I mean, is he making any sort of recovery from the injury to his back.'

'We-ell, Sir James seems to think time and treatment will work wonders. Sir James Trevor, you know. Of course, if anyone can do anything, he can. He's simply wonderful.' The nurse evidently had a very personal admiration for the surgeon.

'Then there's not much danger now of his not walking again?'

The nurse shrugged and remarked conventionally that one must always hope. With which excellent sentiment Virginia agreed.

'I'll look in again before I go to bed,' Virginia said.

Then she went downstairs once more to write her somewhat difficult letter to Richard.

How little and how much was she to say? How did Richard really regard these things? 'These things' meaning living with a man to whom you were not married, of course.

In the end she decided to take her cue from what Jessica had said to that nice cousin of hers. Why not pretend—for at any rate as long as was possible—that she was employed here in Jason Kent's house as some sort of secretary?

It would not be an easy pretence, but well worth trying. After all, it was not at all necessary to the success of their schemes that Richard should think her engaged on a life of vice. Very much the reverse, in fact, if she was to make quite sure that he would accept money from her.

Virginia drew her writing pad towards her and wrote, 'Dear Richard,' rather slowly. Then she carefully inscribed Jessica Young's address at the top of the page.

After that, it was not so difficult. She dashed into a fairly convincing account of how she had had some heart-to-heart talks with Jason while he was in their house (representing him as a slightly eccentric millionaire, she found, on reading the letter over). She explained that he was good enough to think her gifts were wasted in Aunt Julia's house ('I hope he doesn't start wondering what on earth my wasted gifts are,' thought Virginia worriedly), and that he had finally offered her a job.

'*I suppose it will be in his office later on,*' she wrote firmly, '*but at the moment, as he's ill, of course I work here in the house. Will you telephone me at the above number, at any time during the day? But if you write, send the letter to 41, Garden Mansions, Hampstead, where I'm staying with Jessica Young.*'

'There's a lie or a half-lie in every other line,' thought Virginia bitterly. But what else was she to do? What else was she to do?

When she had sealed it up in the envelope and addressed it, she rang the bell. Her first impulse had been to throw on her coat and run out and look for a post box herself. But perhaps that was the wrong way of doing things in this house.

The servant who answered her ring said that, certainly, someone would go to post the letter at once.

'Is there still a collection tonight?' Virginia asked.

'Oh, yes, madam.' He sounded rather as though he would have arranged a special one for her, if not. 'The last post goes at eight o'clock.'

'Thank you.' She turned away again, relieved to know that Richard would get the letter before he left for his office in the morning, and was almost sure to telephone to her before the day was out. Then at least she would know how she stood so far as he was concerned.

There was nothing else to do now except read until it was time to go to bed.

She looked round the room. On a side-table were some papers and magazines, several of them looking as though they had not been opened since they came from the shop.

The first she picked up proved to be exclusively concerned with Stock Exchange news—she supposed it was delivered regularly and lay there unopened whilst Jason was ill—but the second was one of the more expensive women's magazines. She picked it up slowly and stood there idly turning the pages, at first without looking at the contents.

This magazine had not been meant for Jason. It must have been ordered for his wife. The lovely, self-possessed Titian-haired creature who had dazzled them all that afternoon only a few weeks ago.

She supposed that—in the eyes of the servants here, for instance—she had 'supplanted' that lovely vision, and she wondered rather how they explained it to themselves, new clothes or no new clothes.

At half-past ten she decided to go to bed.

Her broken night and the early rising were beginning to tell, in spite of all the excitement and anxiety, and she felt intensely weary.

As she went upstairs she was reminded of the weeks that Jason Kent had spent in their house and how she had gone in almost every evening to see how he was. It seemed only natural that he should be in the same house with her again. So movingly natural that she wondered how she would bear it when these months were over and she was no longer there.

She opened his door quietly, and the nurse looked up at once.

But it was not only the nurse who noticed her entry this time.

'Is that you, darling?' There was lazy affection in every syllable of the rather drowsy greeting from the bed.

It startled Virginia as nothing else had ever startled her in her life before. She knew the next second that it was simply for the benefit of the nurse, but that didn't seem to make any very great difference. Jason had called her 'darling', and in a tone she had never expected to hear from him in support of *any* masquerade.

'Yes.' She recovered her composure somehow and came over to the bed.

Behind her, she knew, the nurse had risen from her chair. But perhaps Jason could see that she was looking their way. If so, he used his opportunity well. Taking Virginia's hands, he pulled her down to him, and the next moment she felt his cool, firm mouth on hers.

She *had* been kissed before, of course. Geoffrey had kissed her quite often in a decorous, tepid manner. But this—this was the first kiss that had ever mattered. If he never kissed her again, it would be the only kiss that ever would matter.

She heard the beating of her heart, the quick intake of

her breath, and then—as something far away and quite unimportant—the closing of the door behind the discreetly departing nurse.

Jason laughed softly.

'Very good for a first attempt, don't you think?'

'Well, I suppose you've had a good deal of practice on other women.'

She didn't know why she said that—sharply and angrily. Perhaps in a sort of self-defence. Perhaps because his flippancy at that moment hurt her almost unbearable, and she wanted to hurt him in return.

'You could be right,' he said cynically. 'Didn't you enjoy it? If you're annoyed, say so.'

'No, I'm not annoyed.' She could not get out much more than a whisper, she found.

'What is it, then?'

'Nothing.'

'My dear, you only hold up conversation when you prevaricate in that ridiculous way. If you're not annoyed because I kissed you—though, heaven knows, that's going to be a very necessary part of the proceedings—what *is* the matter?'

'It's just—'

'Yes?'

'It was such a—a very nice kiss and then, to have you laugh about it—'

She saw the utmost astonishment on his face for a moment, and then he laughed. She had never seen him laugh like that before—the real tenderness that softened those smiling eyes, the warmth and light and pleasure that changed his tired face entirely.

'I never met anything like you! Come here and kiss me again. This time I won't laugh.'

'It doesn't matter—' she began.

'Come,' he said imperiously.

She bent down and he kissed her gently, and warmly as she had not imagined he could kiss anyone. She felt herself responding to him.

'All right now?' he asked softly as he broke away.

'Oh, yes.'

'Go along to bed then and sleep well.'

'And you too.'

'Thank you. Don't come and see me until tomorrow afternoon. The doctor is coming to see me in the morning, and I shan't be fit company for you until after lunch.'

'Why not?' She spoke rather anxiously.

'Because he hurts me a good deal and it makes me very bad-tempered,' he explained with a grimace.

'I shouldn't mind.'

'No? Well, I should. Go and amuse yourself some other way.'

'There isn't any——'

'Well, go out and spend money or something. That's always amusing. Do you want any?'

'No, thank you.' Virginia was rather shocked by the casual way he always seemed ready to throw money about.

'Then goodnight.'

'Goodnight, Jason.'

And she went away then to her lovely bedroom.

CHAPTER SEVEN

VIRGINIA slept dreamlessly. Afterwards, she was surprised to find *how* tranquilly she had slept, that first night in Jason Kent's house.

'I must be either more courageous or more callous than I imagined,' she told herself.

There was no sound at all from the room next door as she bathed and dressed, so she supposed she had better do just what she had been told, and leave him alone until after lunch.

She went downstairs to breakfast, having refused the suggestion that she should have it served in her room. And just as she had finished her meal, Richard telephoned.

It was all she could do not to rush excitedly to the telephone when the servant summoned her, and when she actually heard his familiar voice at the other end, she could only say:

'Oh, Richard——I'm so glad to hear you!'

'I'm glad to hear you too, Virginia. Look here——it's the most extraordinary thing——'

'Yes, I know. But I'll explain about it all when I see you.'

'No. I mean it's an extraordinary thing your turning up in London to-day, of all days. I've got a stupendous piece of news for you. I can't tell you by phone. I'm speaking from the office, and people keep on popping in and out. But I must see you. Can you meet me at six this evening? Do you get out by then?'

'Get out?' She could not understand what he meant for a moment. Then she remembered that she was supposed to

92

be working more or less office hours. 'Oh, yes. Yes, of course I'll meet you. Where? How wonderful to think of having a real talk! Isn't it exciting about my being here?'

'Fine. But just wait until you hear what I have to tell you. Now, can you find your way to a place called The White Lion? It's a little corner café, just off the King's Road, where the coffee's really good. It's quite near where you're working. You turn——'

'I'll take a taxi,' Virginia interrupted. She was not going to run any risk of missing him.

The slight pause showed her how astonished he was.

'A *taxi*! I say, you're throwing the first week's salary about a bit, aren't you?'

'Oh, well—' She laughed rather nervously. 'Anyway, don't bother, I'll find it.'

'All right. Six o'clock. I must go now—we're not really supposed to have personal calls.'

She said good-bye and rang off. Then she sat by the telephone for a minute or two, sunk in thought.

How odd! Richard seemed only passingly interested in the enormous change which had taken place in her life. This 'news' of his simply ruled out what had happened to her. He was rather like that, of course—passionately interested in whatever he was doing at the moment, to the exclusion of everything else.

Still, it made one feel a bit flat to find that a positive revolution in one's life was classed as no more than a pleasant coincidence because it brought one to London at a time when he happened to want a confidante!

Oh, well, perhaps it was natural for a boy to see things like that. And anyway, it wasn't as though he understood (or must be allowed to understand) the real state of affairs. His sister, who didn't like the country, had got a job in Town. That would be the way it would appear to him.

And a good thing, too. It was going to make explanations easier than she had anticipated.

She put on her coat then and went out. That was what Jason had told her to do, and she supposed she had better get to know something of the neighbourhood in which she was going to live.

He had told her to 'spend some money,' too, she remembered with a smile. It seemed to be his fixed idea that women were never very happy unless they were doing that. Presumably his wife was responsible for that theory.

Virginia wondered on what women like Ginette Kent spent their money. Clothes mostly, she supposed.

Well, she herself had bought all the clothes she needed for the moment, so there was nothing to be done about that.

According to Aunt Julia's rule, you bought clothes when they were necessary in order to keep you actually decent. Otherwise, you kept your money in your purse—that was all. And Virginia was finding it very difficult to discard that theory in favour of an inconsequential extravagance which began with nothing more than 'I like that' and ended with one buying whatever 'that' might be.

She headed for Knightsbridge, and she paused from time to time to look in the windows of shops where, she supposed, Mrs Kent had spent a good deal of her money.

It was while she was gazing with absorbed pleasure at a window full of carved amber and jade that an unmistakably delighted voice exclaimed beside her:

'Hello! Do you mean to say your dragon allows you to go shop-gazing in the morning? I never heard of such a thing!'

Virginia turned with a very real pleasure, too.

'Hello, Clive. I thought one never met people one knew in London.'

'One never does,' he assured her seriously. 'This must have been very specially arranged by Fate.'

Virginia laughed, found that he was still holding the

hand she had given him, and rather hastily withdrew it.

'Have you really got time off?' he wanted to know. 'Or are you on some errand for your lord and master?'

'Oh, no, I'm off until after lunch. I was just—looking around I've seldom been in London, you know, and most of it is new to me.'

'Is it?' He looked at her with that smiling admiration quite plain in his clear grey eyes. 'I suppose you wouldn't like—I say, do let me show you round a bit, and then let's have lunch together. Would you like that?'

Virginia hesitated.

She *would* like it. Like it enormously, she found. It was just a little melancholy going round like this in a strange place entirely alone, and a lunch with this charming, engaging cousin of Jessica's would be much nicer than another solitary meal in that magnificent dining-room. But was it all right for her to accept an invitation like this in the circumstance? Would Jason mind?

'What's the difficulty? Are they expecting you for lunch? You could phone and say you were staying out, after all. And I'll see that you're back in good time for whatever your after-lunch appointment is.'

She *could* phone, of course; it was quite true. And Jason had told her not to come near him until after lunch.

'I'll come.' She smiled suddenly as she made up her mind.

'Good girl! Let's find a phone box, and then we can enjoy ourselves.'

It was he who found the telephone box, of course. He, too, who found the telephone number—a good deal amused to discover that she did not know her own business phone number yet.

Virginia telephoned to explain about not being in to lunch, and the calm, 'Very good, madam,' in reply implied that she was entirely free to do whatever she liked.

'All right?' Clive Grove took her arm lightly as she came

out of the telephone box. And, perhaps because she felt very happy and very much out to enjoy herself, she not only allowed him to do so, but very slightly returned the pressure on her arm.

She found he had left his car nearby, and he drove her slowly through the Park, letting her enjoy the sunshine and the space and the green to her heart's content.

Then, turning, he drove her through Piccadilly and Charing Cross and the Strand, pointing out the places of interest on the way, and when they reached the edge of the City, he parked the car in one of the very few streets where one may park cars, and proceeded to show her the quiet, quaint charm of the Inns of Court.

They lunched at a place in Soho—Bohemian enough to intrigue Virginia, but conventional enough to supply excellent food. Her companion was well-known there, she saw, and he chose the meal with discrimination.

As they lingered over their coffee, he glanced at his watch and smiled.

'Plenty of time for me to drive you back, for your afternoon's work.'

'Oh, you needn't take me right to the house——'

'But of course!'

'No—really, I'd rather not. It—it would be better for me to arrive alone.' She felt nervously sure of that.

'No followers allowed, eh?' He seemed amused but inclined to yield now.

'Something like that.'

'Very well. Where shall I drop you?'

'Oh—the shop where you found me, I think. I can find my way back from there quite easily.'

He smiled.

'I'm beginning to think this Jason Kent story a bit of a myth,' he declared. 'I believe——'

'What—what do you mean?' She was terribly startled.

'Well, there's a sort of mystery about you. You appear from nowhere and you go back into nowhere. Besides, you're not like any other girl I ever met.'

Jason had said something like that. She smiled a little.

'I'm sorry, I don't mean to be a mystery.'

'Oh, don't apologise!' he assured her. 'It's very fascinating. If you were a character in one of my books you would be the crux of the mystery, you know. Only you're much more interesting than anyone in my books.'

Virginia slightly shook her head. But it was fun to be assured one was interesting—even fascinating.

He made no trouble after that about leaving her before they reached Jason Kent's house, but deposited her nearby as she wished.

'When am I going to see you again?' he wanted to know.

'I don't—really know.'

'Don't you know what off-time you have yet?'

'No.'

'Well then, if I give you my telephone number, will you promise to ring me up when you have some spare time?'

'Yes.' Virginia took the card he gave her and put it in her bag. 'I promise.'

She shook hands with him then, thanked him for his kindness, and turned rather hurriedly away. Her thoughts were already running on ahead of her.

Jason—how was he? Had he had a bad morning? Was he wondering when she would come? Even looking forward to her coming? She felt now that she had left him too long.

Her own morning had been so gay and carefree, full of springtime happiness and the sheer pleasure of having a good time. But he had to lie there in his magnificent bedroom, with only the unwished-for coming of the doctor to break the monotony, hardly knowing or caring whether it were winter still or spring.

As though by instinct, Virginia stopped at that point

beside the window of a florist's shop she was passing.

She had never bought flowers for anyone before, never had the money to do so, but she knew that great bunch of heavy, dew-damped violets must be expensive. Still, she had money. He had even told her to spend it.

At that moment Virginia really sensed the full pleasure of having money to spend. She could spend it on him.

As she entered the shop a very exclusive-looking young woman drifted towards her.

'Yes, madam?'

'The violets—how much are they, please?'

'Fifty pence a bunch, madam.'

'No, all of them, I mean.'

'Oh.' The girl gathered them up in her hands and began to count them. 'There are ten bunches, madam. Five pounds in all.'

Five pounds' worth of flowers! It was preposterous— and yet she wanted them for him. Not just a few, but that extravagant bunch which the girl could hardly hold in both her hands.

'I'll take them,' Virginia said. 'Will you put them all together in one bunch, please?'

The girl took them away to the back of the shop to arrange them, and Virginia stood there gazing unseeingly at early daffodils and mimosa and hyacinths in pots.

Five pounds' worth of violets! Aunt Julia would have thought she ought to be certified.

But she was so happy about them. She had never been quite so happy about anything in her life as she was about the great fragrant bunch of violets which the girl presently handed to her in exchange for a five-pound note.

She hurried home. When she got into the house, she carried them straight upstairs. She didn't even wait to take off her coat, but went into Jason's room as she was. He was lying propped up in bed, and looked up languidly from a book he had been reading.

'Hello, Virginia.'

'Hello.'

She hardly knew how to explain her presence there in her outdoor things, with the bunch of flowers in her hands. She had no idea that to the sick man she seemed, as she crossed the room, like light and colour personified.

Without a word, Virginia held out the violets to him.

'For me?' He looked puzzled, amused, and then quite extraordinarily touched, as he put down his book and rather slowly took the flowers in his hands. He held them a little awkwardly, looking at them rather than at her.

'They're lovely. Where did you get them?'

'I—bought them. For you. You said I was to go out and spend some money, so I did.'

'You spent your money on—me?' There was an odd note in his voice.

'Well, it's really your money, of course, isn't it?' she said literally.

'No, my dear. The money was yours, to buy what would give *you* pleasure.'

'You—you like them, don't you?' She hardly knew what to make of this.

'Yes, I like them.' He had looked up again immediately and replied almost laconically. He didn't even thank her in words. But she knew instinctively that she had given him the keenest pleasure. A puzzling, unfamiliar pleasure, no doubt, but none the less acceptable for that.

'Now.' He was entirely himself again. 'Tell me what you've been doing with yourself all day. Oh, take off your things and sit down. You're at home, you know.' He said that with his old mocking air, but not with any idea of hurting her, she saw.

Virginia put her coat on a chair and sat down on the side of the bed, facing him.

'Shall I put the violets in water?'

'No, leave them here for a moment. Did you spend all the morning finding violets for me?'

'Oh, no!' She laughed a little. 'I've been having a morning of sightseeing and enjoying myself. I met someone I know——'

'I thought you didn't know anyone in London.'

'Well, I didn't. I mean—hardly anyone until yesterday. When I went to buy my new clothes, I looked up an acquaintance of mine—a fashion artist I had met when she was in the country last summer——'

'Oh, a woman?' He interrupted again as though he had a right to question her, and she thought very little got past him, but somehow it was very different from the searching catechisms of Aunt Julia.

'Oh, yes—a woman. Jessica Young is her name. She introduced me to a cousin of hers while I was in her flat. A man called Clive Grove. He writes detective novels. And funnily enough, he saw me this morning while I was looking in a shop window.'

'So he took you sightseeing?'

'Yes.'

'Hm. A man who uses his opportunities, evidently.'

'Ye-es.' She was more doubtful how to reply that time, and after a moment she asked: 'Do you mind?'

'Mind? That you should go out with him, you mean?' She nodded.

'No,' he said, with another of those odd glances at her. 'No, I don't mind. Is he—nice?'

'Oh, very.'

'What type?'

She found that rather difficult.

'He doesn't seem to take life very seriously, but somehow'—she looked reflective—'somehow, I think he would be a good friend to have in an emergency.

'He isn't engaged to this—cousin of his?'

'No. At least, I don't think so. No, I'm sure not,' she added after a moment, certain that Jessica would have mentioned such a circumstance.

'So you enjoyed yourself very much?'

'Very much.' Virginia smiled at the recollection of how much. 'I suppose,' she added slowly, 'it was partly that I've never been out with a man before. Not *really* out, I mean.'

'The excellent Geoffrey didn't——'

'Oh, well, going to see a film in a country cinema with Geoffrey wasn't quite the same thing, you know.'

'No,' he agreed. 'No, I suppose that would hardly come under the heading of "going out with a man". So this was your first real flutter?'

'Yes,' she admitted.

He was silent for a while.

'Richard telephoned to me this morning,' she ventured presently, feeling that perhaps he expected to know about everything she was doing. 'I wrote to him last night explaining—explaining——'

'What did you explain this time, Virginia?' That faintly cynical look came back into his eyes.

'I said I had a job here. In a way that's true.'

'Perfectly true,' he agreed gravely. 'So you don't propose to let him know the exact state of affairs?'

'No. Oh, no. He probably wouldn't accept money from me if I did that.'

'I'm glad to hear it.'

'What did you say?'

'It's of no consequence. He was very pleased, of course, to know you were here?'

'Yes, delighted.' Perhaps Virginia was all the more

emphatic about that because Richard's welcome had *not* been quite so ecstatic as all that. 'But he says he has some exciting news, too.'

'Promotion in his office?' Jason suggested.

'N-no, I don't think he'd regard that as exciting,' Virginia admitted. 'As a matter of fact, it may not be anything very much. Richard's still very much a little boy in some things. He gets wildly excited about whatever interests him at the moment.'

'So this interested him even more than the arrival of his sister in London?'

'Well, perhaps it's natural for a boy to feel his sister isn't quite the most important thing on earth.'

'But not for a sister to feel the same about her brother?'

Virginia didn't answer that. She was rather shocked to be facing the fact—in so many words—that Richard was no longer the most important thing on earth to *her*.

'He didn't tell you on the phone about this interesting development?'

'No. He was speaking from the office, so he couldn't be explicit. But I'm meeting him this evening at six at— Oh!' she stopped. 'Is it all right my making arrangements like this without asking you?' She drew her straight brows together in a perplexed frown.

'My dear Virginia'—he smiled—'I could scarcely expect you to hang about this house doing nothing, simply because I happen to be ill in one of the bedrooms.'

'No.' She supposed it was her duty, all the same, to do something which should give the impression to the nurse and servants at least that she was very much more to Jason Kent than she should be. Was she not being paid for just that?

'So you're meeting Richard this evening?'

'Yes.'

'Are you going to find further explanations a trifle difficult?'

'No, I don't think so.' She was not really quite certain about that.

'Well, I should stick to the story of an office job, if I were you,' he said carelessly.

It surprised her a little that he should say that. She could not remember a single other occasion when he had offered her definite advice about her own affairs.

She murmured, 'Oh, I shall, of course.' But she wondered very much why he had bothered to say it.

She even thought about it again when she was on her way to meet Richard that evening—but only with passing attention this time. Because, of course, now that the meeting was so near, it was very difficult to think of anything else.

What would Richard think of her news? And what, she wondered, was she going to think of his?

She found her way to the meeting-place on foot in the end. He was already there when she arrived, standing outside the café, his hands thrust deep into the pockets of his raincoat, his attention very much occupied by something that was passing on the river.

Even when she saw him at a distance, it seemed to Virginia that her heart rushed out to meet him. He looked so young and slight and defiant, standing there in the cheap raincoat which Aunt Julia had reluctantly included in his outfit.

'Richard!' She was right behind him now, and at her exclamation he swung round to greet her.

'Hello, Virginia.' He hugged her. 'I say!' He held her a little away from him. 'Aunt Julia did you a good deal better than me on a business outfit, didn't she?'

'Oh, yes. Never mind now. It looks more expensive than it is, I dare say.' She was in something of a hurry to change the subject. 'Come on, let's go in and have coffee and get warm.'

They went into the café together, Virginia still gripping his arm with nervous, affectionate fingers.

There was hardly anyone else in the place, and they took their cups of coffee from the counter and sat down.

'Oh, this is *nice*!' Virginia smiled at him.

'Yes, isn't it? You look well, Virginia.'

'I am. And you?' She examined him with loving, anxious eyes. He was pale and there were slight unhappy lines round his mouth. But his eyes just then were sparkling with eagerness and a glowing satisfaction.

'I'm all right. Guess what, Virginia——' And then, as though he were too impatient to await her guessing, 'I'm leaving the office!'

'Leaving!' Virginia stared at him. She wanted to say: 'Yes, of course. But *I'm* arranging that. How did you know?'

But something in his face held her silent.

He took a quick gulp at the hot coffee, and then pushed it aside, leaning his elbows on the table so that his eager face, was quite close to hers.

'I've got my chance, Jinny! Such a chance as you can't imagine!' Even the old, childish form of her name slipped out. 'I didn't tell you—I've been going to evening classes at the art school near my office. David Parkington comes there once a week to give a special lesson to the favoured few. You know—David Parkington, the painter.'

'Yes, I know.' She nodded slowly, but she managed to say the words in quite an eager tone.

'Of course, I wasn't one of his pupils—not far enough advanced—but he happened to see some of my work. I don't know how, even now—just the merest chance, I believe. He sent for me and talked to me for ages about my work. Said it was amazingly promising and quite individual.

Oh, all the things one's always longed to hear and never *has* heard. He said I ought to give up my whole time to learning my job properly. And, of course, he evidently thought he only had to say it and I'd do it.'

'He's a very rich man himself, isn't he?' Virginia interrupted. 'They always think everything's possible.'

'Yes, yes.' Richard brushed the generalisation aside. He was interested only in his hero. 'He's got a very big income, besides what he makes from his work. That's how he's going to manage it.'

'Manage what?'

'Well, I'm just going to *tell* you, if you wouldn't interrupt.'

'All right. Sorry.'

'I just had to explain everything then. About having a job I loathed and not being able to study at all, except in this scrappy way at evening classes. He said it was absurd. Oh, I wish Aunt Julia could just have heard him!'

'It wouldn't have changed her views an inch,' Virginia declared with conviction.

'No, but it might have done her good,' retorted Richard viciously. 'Anyway, he just got to work on smoothing out the difficulties right away. He's got a big, rambling house overlooking Wimbledon Common, you know—lives there with a maiden aunt or sister or something. And just imagine, Jinny!—I'm to go and live there, too, and study with him! He's letting me have two rooms of my own there. They're at the end of a long corridor, set apart from the rest of the house, because, of course, he wouldn't want me around all the time.'

'Do you mean he's going to *keep* you? Find everything?'

'Yes. I know it sounds a bit boastful to repeat what he really said, Jinny. But he told me he wasn't going to have a talent like mine wasted because of a mere question of board and lodging. He's going to put me in for the Enderby

Scholarship. That would mean a year in Paris and a year in Florence, if I got it. I'll work like hell. I *can* work, you know,' he added a little pathetically, 'when it's stuff I can do and love. Oh, Jinny, just think of the chance! the—happiness! Sometimes I wonder if it's really happened or if I've just gone out of my mind.'

She wondered too if it had really happened or if *she* had 'gone out of her mind.'

What was Richard saying? Oh, not just the words, but the implications.

He didn't need her. He didn't need her and her absurd plans to get money, after all. He had found his own fantastic chance himself.

The overwhelming reason for Jason even suggesting his plan—and for her accepting it—simply no longer existed. No wonder she sat there staring at Richard, until he exclaimed with eager impatience:

'Well, Virginia, don't you think it's marvellous? Haven't you anything to say?'

'Yes. It's—wonderful. Almost unbelievable. It—takes your breath away—makes it difficult to say anything.'

'I know, I know! That's how I felt about it. The evening after it was all settled, I walked and walked along the Embankment, trying to convince myself that it was real. I could have stopped everyone I met and told them, I was so excited. Only there was no one who would really understand. That's why I'm so glad you're here, Jinny. It's lovely to have you to tell.'

She was touched by that at once.

'Oh, Richard, I *am* more glad than I can possibly say, you know. Tell me some more. When are you leaving the office? You're still there, aren't you?'

'Oh, yes. I forgot to explain that. I had to give a fortnight's notice, you know. Those were the terms of my appointment, and I didn't want to leave even the office in an unnecessary cloud of smoke,' he added ingenuously. 'The time's up at the end of this week. I hadn't written home to tell you, for fear you let it slip to Aunt Julia. And I don't mean to tell *her* until the whole thing's settled beyond her interference.'

'Of course not.' Virginia slowly stirred her coffee and gazed into her cup.

'Richard, if you—if you don't like the feeling of being entirely dependent on this Mr Parkington, I can let you have some money now. That's what *I* wanted to tell *you*—that you needn't bother about things any longer. I'm earning a very good salary, and I dare say you'd rather I——'

'No, really, that's all right.' He interrupted her at once, putting aside even that modified offer. 'You see, he's got this idea of doing the job himself—taking the most personal interest in setting me on my feet. He's rather eccentric, the kind to like the feeling that he can work miracles, if you know what I mean. I think it would be a mistake—psychologically, that is—to turn up now and suggest that it wasn't very necessary, after all. He might lose interest.'

'That sounds rather petty,' Virginia objected.

'It's nothing of the sort!' Richard was affronted. 'It's his way of doing things, that's all.'

'Think so?' Virginia looked back at her brother with troubled eyes. He was very dear and absurd, with his talk of 'psychological mistakes' and his certainty that only he could manage this strange and wonderful situation.

But then perhaps he was right. Perhaps it was only that in her heart she *wanted* him to be wrong, because it hurt so strangely to find he simply didn't need the surprise gift she had for him.

'You don't—mind taking money from a stranger like that?' she suggested, but this time a little more diffidently than she usually addressed her young brother.

'Oh, *no*, Virginia! Why should I? It's not an unknown

thing for a big artist or musician or someone like that to
take on a protégé because he thinks the result will justify
his judgment. The only thing is that it never seemed
possible that it could happen to oneself.'

'No. I see.'

'It's very sweet of you, Jinny.' He recollected himself a
little now that all the explanations and arguments were over.
'You always are so generous. But, as a matter of fact, I dare
say you'll be glad of your whole salary, particularly at first.
This place runs away with a lot of money, and Aunt Julia
doesn't exactly start one off in clover, does she?'

'No. But I could have managed. I *could* always manage,
even now, if you needed things.' She wondered if it sounded
pathetically silly that she wanted so much to find something
she could give him.

Apparently not, because he assured her with cheerful
frankness:

'That's all right, Jinny. It's very nice of you, but I don't
imagine I shall need anything. To tell the truth, I should
feel worse living on your first earnings than accepting this
offer of a very rich man on a sort of business-cum-friend-
ship basis. I can repay him by working so hard that I'm
a credit to his teaching. And if I *could* win this scholarship,
of course, I'd be off his hands at once, and at the same time
he'd feel that his judgment had been upheld.'

'I see,' Virginia said again. There didn't seem much else
to say.

Richard drank his coffee, satisfied to turn his attention to
it, now that the great business of unloading his news had
been attended to.

Presently he looked up again, however, and remarked:

'This must be an awfully good job you've got, Virginia.
You talk already as though you're quite used to having
money to spend. And yet, goodness knows, we neither of us
had much practice in that line.' And he laughed.

'Oh.' Virginia forced a smile too. 'Yes, it *is* a good job. Our—well, our luck as a family seems to be in just now.'

Richard agreed cheerfully.

'It's this chap who had the car accident, you said in your letter.'

'Yes. We—got quite friendly while I was nursing him. Of course, he could see some things for himself about Aunt Julia's weird ways, and in the end I suppose I told him a good deal more than I meant to. You do, you know, when someone is unexpectedly interested and sympathetic.'

'You bet!' Richard was pleased to be able to confirm this from his own happy experience. 'And so he offered you a job in London?'

'Yes.'

'You haven't any qualifications much, have you?' Richard spoke with brotherly candour.

'Well, no not in the way of specialised training, that is. But I suppose he thought I showed glimmerings of common sense, and he could see I was used to doing what I was told, and he decided I was worth training and giving a chance.'

'Funny we should both strike our lucky patch together.'

'Very funny,' agreed Virginia rather drearily.

'Is he an old man?'

'Oh, *no*! In his mid thirties—I don't know. It's rather difficult to tell while he's ill and a bit—haggard.'

Richard nodded without interest.

'Married?' he enquired presently.

'Yes.' Virginia felt they were approaching dangerous ground. 'Why?'

'Oh, nothing really. One just likes to know it's all fair and above-board, that's all. It's unusual for someone to offer a girl anything like that out of the blue.'

She felt very cold, in spite of the pleasant fire.

'It's perfectly—fair and above-board.' She took a quick breath. 'But of course, as you can imagine, Aunt Julia draws all sorts of—of spiteful conclusions. I shouldn't be terribly surprised if she wrote to you more or less accusing me of going off with Mr Kent in quite—disreputable circumstances. You know the sort of thing she thinks and says.'

Richard nodded feelingly.

'But it's—it's all right, really. And anyway'—she even managed a not very convincing little laugh—'I can look after myself.'

'I dare say,' Richard agreed. 'Though I sometimes think Aunt Julia didn't exactly bring us up in a way to show us how to take care of ourselves. I'm occasionally surprised to find I wasn't made a fool of in one way or another when I first came to London. Just luck, I suppose.'

'Yes,' Virginia agreed faintly. And there was silence again. On his side it was the silence of contentment and a happy visualising of the future. On hers it was blank and bewildered and empty.

At last he said:

'I'm afraid I'll have to go. I'm due at Wimbledon for dinner. Of course I haven't had a chance to explain about you yet, so you don't mind if I—if I go off without you.'

'Of course not.' She roused herself. 'You mustn't give him the idea that he's taking on the whole family, simply because he's being kind to you.'

'No—of course not.' Richard smiled. 'Only I'm sure you'll get an invitation by and by.' He evidently regarded that as the height of human happiness, and Virginia smiled gratefully.

'That would be lovely,' she agreed.

'Where did you say this Jessica Young lived? Hampstead? Better get the tube.'

'But I'm not——' She stopped, remembering just in time that she was supposed to be living with Jessica. 'Oh, yes—yes, of course. I expect that will be best. Thank you, Richard.'

'Here's my bus coming.' He kissed her hastily. 'Goodbye, Jinny. It's been lovely seeing you. I'll let you know as soon as possible how things turn out and we'll meet again.'

'Goodbye. Yes, do let's.'

He got on the bus, and the conductor rang the bell. Virginia stood there for a moment, waving her hand and smiling in a bravely casual way.

Then she walked off into the darkness, which seemed to press in upon her, back to Jason Kent's home.

CHAPTER EIGHT

So that was that!

Had anyone ever been a more complete and utter fool? She rather thought not.

The urgent motive behind all the mad impulse of the last weeks had been to rescue Richard. There had been the relief of escape for herself as well, but she would never have— what was it?—thrown her cap over the windmill for that.

It had been for Richard! And now he simply didn't need it.

She had a vague idea that it served her right. That if one deliberately upset one's sense of values—did something wrong for the sake of setting something right—one must expect disaster.

But then what was right and what was wrong in this tangle?

She knew she would go home to him now. How absurd to wander these monotonous, unknown streets moping over Richard who no longer needed her, when all the time Jason was waiting at home, ill and alone.

After a while she found her way—discovered, in fact, that she as not so very far from home. Then she smiled a little to herself. Strange, but she already thought of Jason Kent's big, quiet house as 'home.'

She even found a soothing, friendly familiarity about the sombre, panelled hall as she came into the house, and she looked round with an almost affectionate pleasure at everything.

It must be past dinner-time by now, she knew, but the servant asked her politely if she had had dinner, or would she like some now.

'No, no, it's all right, thank you. I don't want anything.' She smiled at him and went quickly upstairs.

It was true. She didn't want anything. She only wanted to be with Jason and talk to him, to see his tired eyes smile just because she came into the room.

She took her outdoor things off and went straight to his room.

He was alone when she entered in answer to his bidding, and for that she was warmly glad. It was so much nicer when the nurse was away—nicer when they didn't even have to have her discreet departure impressed somewhat embarrassingly on their consciousness.

'Oh, I'm so glad to see you!' She came over and sat down in her usual place on the side of the bed, with perhaps less reserve than she had ever shown before.

'How very gratifying.' His half-mocking smile was on her, but she thought he looked serious behind that.

'I've seen Richard.'

'And explained—more or less?'

'Well, no. To tell the truth, there was hardly anything much in the way of explanation needed. He quite easily accepted the idea that I was working here as a secretary.'

'Great heavens!'

'Why? What do you mean?'

'I was only wondering,' he told her dryly, 'how the Richards of this world imagine that men in my position build up a business career. By employing entirely inexperienced and unqualified young women in the important position of secretary, I suppose?'

'Oh.' Virginia laughed and coloured slightly. 'It does sound idiotic, of course, but I don't expect he was paying much attention, anyway. He was frightfully excited because something marvellous has happened to him. You know David Parkington, the artist?'

'Not personally, I'm glad to say. An indescribably self-satisfied person in a large hat, if I remember rightly.'

'Well'—she was slightly dashed—'I don't know about that. But he's very successful, isn't he?'

'Is he? I'm not supposed to know about these things, being merely a Philistine of the business world, remember. However'—he smiled slightly at her perplexed expression —'we'll take it that he's all of that. At any rate, he's very successful in his own line—which is the part that I can appreciate. Go on. I suppose he's taken an interest in your brother?'

'Yes. How did you guess that?'

'A little simple deduction from the awed way in which you breathed his name. Besides, one of life's little ironies.'

'I don't understand.'

'It doesn't matter. Go on.'

'Well, it's the most overwhelming interest that he's taken in Richard. He wants to train him, take full responsibility for him until he's on his feet—everything.'

'Board and lodging thrown in, I take it?'

'Yes, exactly.'

'And he's perfectly willing to accept?'

'Well, yes, he is.'

'Really.' He sounded suddenly weary of the conversation.

'You disapprove?'

'My dear girl, it isn't for me to approve or disapprove. I've never been an artistic genius and don't know what it feels like to be one. Perhaps the artistic urge transcends everything else. It seems a lot to be taking from a stranger for nothing, that's all.'

There was a short pause. Then Virginia said honestly:

'I feel rather the same, to tell the truth. But he seems perfectly satisfied and determined himself. He even said that he will feel better accepting such an offer from a rich man than he would have if he'd accepted anything from my first earnings. That was how I had to put it to him, of course,' she added, in hasty parenthesis.

'Of course. Well, perhaps he's right, Virginia. In any case, it isn't a point we shall any of us stress if Richard attains to fame and fortune. These are the things which sink conveniently into a vague background them.'

'Yes.' She was not sure that it was as unimportant as all that. If a question of principle were really involved—

'And so, Virginia,' he said slowly, 'Richard no longer needs rescuing?'

'No.' She stared rather hard at the heavy silk bedspread.

'That's rather awkward for you, isn't it?'

'No, not—awkward exactly. It's just disappointing.' Her voice sank almost to a whisper. 'I meant to do quite a lot for him. I'd have liked to. Only—' She stopped and bit her lip hard. 'Well, never mind. It's over now.'

There was a long silence. Then Jason said quietly, a little dryly:

'So is your reason for entering on this arrangement with me over now?'

'Oh, no!' She looked up quickly. 'You don't think I'd back out now, just because my part of it hasn't worked out quite as expected?'

'I wasn't thinking of it in terms of your backing out, Virginia. I was thinking that, curiously enough, events are perhaps arranging themselves to suit certain altered circumstances.'

'What do you mean?' For some reason she could not define she suddenly felt deadly afraid.

'I mean, my dear, that, however you choose to look at it, you *have* no longer an overwhelming reason for generally messing up your life. I know that, as you say, you would still keep to the bargain, if I wished it. Just as, believe me, I should quite ruthlessly hold you to it—if I wished it.'

'*If* you wished it? I don't understand. Do you mean that you don't wish it?' She had never felt anything like this chill of despair.

'Exactly. You don't have to simulate dismay, you know. It would be so much more logical to show considerable relief, and, I can assure you, my feelings will not be hurt.'

'But you don't understand! I'm *willing* to go on with it. It wasn't only for Richard. It was for myself. My own chance of escape from the sort of life I was living.'

It sounded such a miserable, tawdry, unworthy reason. But what else could she plead?

Nothing, nothing, nothing!

He would not even be interested in the one inescapable reason that bound her to this bargain. She couldn't say to him: 'I love you. Please let us go on with this.' He would merely be embarrassed—if it were possible for such a cynic to feel embarrassed—and the end would be humiliation unutterable.

She forced herself to look up and meet his eyes. He looked calm and unmoved as usual.

'We're talking rather at cross-purposes, Virginia. You think that some sort of belated nobility of purpose has descended on me, and that I'm gallantly releasing you from your bargain at some cost to my own wishes. I hate to spoil such a bright picture—but, frankly, the halo won't fit. The plain and brutal truth is that Ginette came here unexpectedly while you were out. We had a long talk together and we've decided we want to make a second attempt to put up with each other. Perhaps we shall be more successful after certain experiences on both sides.'

The blow was so terrific—so unexpected—that for a moment the whole room went black around her. The surprise and disappointment which Richard had loosed on her had been a little squib compared to this bombshell, and this time her whole world rocked.

She had to say something. And out of the depths of her misery and despair there stumbled the one silly little sentence:

'I see.'

Perhaps even Jason was a little put out by her blankness. At any rate, he evidently thought he knew the reason for it, because he went on almost immediately:

'Of course, I have no intention of leaving you stranded so that you're thrown back on your aunt. You undertook this business partly to oblige me, and, even if it suits neither of us now to carry it through, at least I don't mean that you shall be at any loss. If you agree, I think the best thing is for you to leave here as soon as possible. I can undertake to silence any small amount of gossip there might have been. And I'll give you a few hundred pounds, so that you can keep yourself while you get some sort of training for a job.'

It was terribly difficult to keep her mind on what he was saying—to follow and look intelligent. But that bit got through to her.

'Oh, no. No, thank you,' she protested hastily. 'I don't want your money. I haven't done anything for it. I don't need it.'

'Don't be ridiculous, Virginia,' he retorted coolly. 'Of course you need it. Besides, you *have* done something for it—left your home and put yourself in a very questionable position. It's not your fault that there hasn't been more for you to do for it, but, on the other hand, you're not receiving anything like the amount of money agreed on for the real job. Many people would demand the whole sum, I suppose. But I won't insult you by suggesting that. I'm merely suggesting a reasonable compromise. Believe me, it's not an excessively generous offer.'

With a bitterness of which she would not have thought herself capable, she threw back his own words at him:

'It seems a lot to be taking from a stranger for nothing, that's all.'

Jason must have been very greatly angered by that, she thought. He looked so white and bleak, and for a moment he said nothing at all. When he replied it was in a singularly expressionless tone.

'I'm not a stranger, my dear, and it was not for nothing. It was for services rendered, if you wish the expression used.'

'Oh, how dare—' She began furiously, but he held up his hand.

'Wait a moment, let's get this straight. And, for heaven's sake, don't let's be emotional about it. If you accept this money, to which you're perfectly entitled on business grounds alone, you'll go out of this house at least with something to face the future—actually with enough to *build* a future, if you use the money sensibly. You can do it. You have enough energy, brains and common sense to make just such a life for yourself as you longed for when you lived with your aunt. If you refuse my offer, what can you do?'

She was silent—for, indeed, what *could* she do?

'You could go back to your aunt, of course—always supposing she would have you, which is not certain—and have a much worse time with her than you ever had before. You haven't deserved that. There's no earthly reason why you should insist on suffering that. Come now, Virginia— please—won't you accept what's not only necessary to you, but honestly owing to you, by every right?'

She knew he was watching her with a sort of angry impatience, waiting for her to reply.

There was no other choice. There was literally no other choice. The only other thing she could do was to go and scrounge from some generous, easily-imposed-on person like Jessica, and hope to be allowed to live on *her* until a job turned up.

But that would be wretchedly unfair to Jessica, while this—this only outraged her own feelings. And there *was* some sort of bitter truth, of course, in what he was saying.

'Very well.' She spoke rather huskily and without looking at him. 'Very well, I will take the money——'

'Good girl!'

'But only as a loan——'

'Oh, don't be absurd!'

'No, I mean it. I'm entitled to keep some sort of pride, however much I may have made a fool of myself.'

'But, child, I've got so *much* money. Don't you know you're welcome to it?'

'And I suppose you enjoy going about throwing money in other people's faces ?'

'Oh, my God!' If she had struck him he could not have looked more white and furious.

'Very well.' His voice was level. 'You shall have the money as a loan, of course. Will you have it now?'

'If you please.' It was she who spoke tonelessly this time, and she never changed her expression as she accepted the cheque from him. It was a horrible moment—so horrible that she could not bring herself to think of its full implications yet.

He too seemed oppressed by the silence, because after a moment he said almost nervously:

'When will you be going, Virginia?'

'Now.'

'Oh, that isn't necessary! To-morrow——'

'Now,' Virginia repeated coldly. 'As soon as I can put on my coat.'

'As you like.' He glanced away almost indifferently.

This was the Jason Kent she had been warned against. This impossible, indifferent creature who cared about nothing now that he had settled his own affairs to his liking.

At one point he had wanted to get rid of his wife, so he had engineered an elaborate deception with some fool of a girl. Then he changed his mind, and didn't want to get rid of her after all, so he paid the fool of a girl to get out of the way again. And it all mattered less than nothing. All except the fact that he had got his own way each time.

It was so callous and cynical, that she felt sick to her very heart.

She got up slowly. This was the end.

'Goodbye.' It sounded sufficiently like her own voice to pass muster.

'Goodbye, Virginia.'

Then turning away, she slowly picked up her coat from the chair, and went out of the room without looking back.

It took scarcely more than ten minutes to pack her things back into the lovely new case and put on her outdoor clothes. It would not have taken even so long as that if her hands had not been shaking so much.

Then she took the case and went quietly out of the room, turning her head away, so that she need not even look at his door.

There was no need to tiptoe down *these* stairs, but she went in nervous dread lest one of the servants should see her.

Oh, they didn't matter, of course. Nothing mattered any longer. But the final humiliation would have been if someone actually saw her creep away from the house—sent packing with bag and baggage.

The case was not heavy, but she set it down for a moment so that she could open the big door quietly. Then she lifted it out on to the step and closed the door behind her.

Twenty-eight hours!—something like that since she had first stood there with her case.

And once more life had changed completely.

She went slowly down the steps and along the side of the dark square. It was a good thing that it was dark, because now she was crying. Quietly, but quite unrestrainedly, so that the tears trickled slowly down her cheeks.

It didn't matter. There was nothing she could care about any longer.

She tried to remember Jason as he had been just now— cold and casual and indifferent, so that she might steel her heart. But it was useless. That was the awful part of it. It was useless.

She could only remember him smiling at her.

But that had not been the real Jason Kent. Just momentary touches of charm which everyone admitted he possessed —but nothing that lasted a moment beyond the point when he suddenly decided he wanted his wife back, and Virginia was no longer useful.

Oh, that was the crux of the matter, of course. No man could be at his best when he was trying to get rid of a woman who stood embarrassingly between him and a reconciliation with his wife.

She set down her case in the shadows and tried to find her handkerchief. It was absurd to go along like this— crying bitterly—even though no one could see her.

She tried forlornly to argue with herself, to tell herself it served her right. What else could she expect? Running off with a man who was not her husband. It needed no Aunt Julia to point out that this had been the original wrong, and that she had only herself to thank for what had followed.

It was poor comfort, however, and picking up her case again, she went slowly on.

The tears had stopped now and, except for an occasional after-sob, she was calm once more. But she was growing cold, and she wondered frightenedly what she was to do.

No doubt there were hotels and boarding-houses to which she could go—but where? She was wandering in a maze of streets now, where every house seemed almost aggressively shuttered against her.

She trudged on until she reached a crossing. Then as she stood there undecided, a taxi drew up by the curb.

'Taxi, madam?'

And, for the second time in two days, she remembered Jessica with a flood of relief. Jessica, who had said she was to come back if things went wrong.

'Yes, please,' Virginia said, and, giving the address, she got wearily into the taxi.

Only when she sat down and found how tired she was did she realise how far she must have walked that evening. However, there was no need to pity herself for that now. It was unimportant. What she had to do was to think out some sort of explanation to give to Jessica.

But what, what, what?

Her tired brain seemed incapable of invention now. Only the most absurd. disjointed thoughts drifted through it—and none of them supplied her with an explanation for Jessica.

Only one thing she clung to with vague thankfulness. Jessica had said something about her having to come back if things went wrong, and then she had promised not to say, 'I told you so.'

Virginia rang the bell.

It was late, of course, to call. Something like ten o'clock she supposed. Jessica might be out. She might have visitors.

The door opened and Clive Grove's voice exclaimed:

'Well, this is nice! Do come in.'

She came in. What else was there to do?

He took her case from her hand, quite as though it were a natural thing for someone to arrive at this time of night, complete with luggage, and in a slightly dazed condition.

'Is Jessica in?'

'No, I'm sorry, she's just gone round to see a friend and I've stayed here to take a phone message she was expecting.

But she won't be long. Come in here and sit down by the fire. Cold, isn't it?'

She didn't answer, and he scarcely seemed to expect her to—simply kept up a soothing trickle of conversation which was designed to cover her stunned bewilderment.

'Have you had any supper?'

'Yes—no. It doesn't matter, thank you.'

'Of course it does. I'll get you some.'

He appeared not to notice how unnerved she was, but went off into the kitchenette with a cheerful injunction to 'get herself warmed through.'

She could hear him whistling as he moved about there and clattered pans.

Slowly the warmth and the rest and the undemanding comfort of it all began to have its effect on her. She felt less dazed, less inclined to shrink back into the shadows and wish she need never come out again.

By the time he came back into the room she was more herself again.

'Here you are. No, don't move. I've put it all on a tray, so you can easily have it beside the fire. I'll have some coffee with you. It always feels like the wrong side of the Zoo if you have to eat in solitary state while someone else looks on.'

Virginia smiled, and watched with real interest while he set down an excellent little meal beside her.

'How nice it looks. You're very good to me.'

'Not a bit of it. You're pretty hungry, aren't you?'

She nodded. Now she came to think of it, she had had nothing solid since lunch, hours ago. Hours? Why, was it only *to-day* that she had had lunch with Clive?

Virginia looked at him with startled blue eyes.

'Was it only to-day that we had lunch together?'

'It was. My lucky day, decidedly—to have you with me for two meals.' He spoke quite brightly, but his eyes, in their turn, looked watchful and concerned.

She didn't say any more, and he let her eat her meal without further conversation, lounging on the rug himself, sipping his coffee, and making a casual remark from time to time, which required only a monosyllable in reply from her. By the time she had finished the meal and handed him back the tray, she was able to give him a very real smile of gratitude.

Clive took the tray into the kitchen and then came back to his seat on the rug.

'Cigarette?'

'No, thank you. I don't smoke.'

She watched while he lit a cigarette. And then it was really impossible to put it off any longer, she supposed.

'I—I think I ought to explain,' she began nervously.

'You don't have to, you know. That is, unless you want to.' He regarded the lighted tip of his cigarette with interest. 'There are more mistakes made in this world by giving explanations than by withholding them, to my way of thinking.'

There was a profound silence while she digested this.

'But don't you think it very peculiar my turning up like this with my suit-case and no explanation?'

'If you feel there are explanations to be made, obviously the person you have to make them to is Jessica. It would be just too bad luck if the fact that I happened to be here at the wrong moment meant you had to make all sorts of reluctant confidences to me, too.'

'I don't think you were here at the wrong moment,' Virginia said soberly. 'I think you were here at just the right moment. I'm wondering what I should have done without you.'

'It was pretty obvious that you'd had a bad knock in some way or another. And the only thing to do for people in that state is to make them comfortable, give them a meal and refrain from badgering them.'

'I see.' She smiled. 'Well, it seems to have worked.'

'Of course. The best theories always do.'

'But, all the same,' Virginia spoke slowly, her eyes very earnestly on the fire, 'all the same, I feel I owe you *some* sort of explanation.'

'No, you don't owe it. But if you *want* to tell me, that's a different thing. Or if there's anything I can do for you about it, of course I'll be only too glad if you will tell me.'

'There's nothing I want you to do about it,' Virginia told him rather gently. 'Only I do want to explain, partly because you've been so good to me, and partly—partly——'

'Because you must talk to someone?'

She nodded.

'Not Jessica?'

'No. I haven't been quite truthful even with her about this business, and—oh, dear, I sometimes think I've told each person a different story!'

'Very bad rule, you know.' He tapped the ash off the end of his cigarette into the fire. 'And anyway, if you'll excuse the compliment, you're a rotten liar. Best thing you can do, Virginia, is to stick to the truth. It's safest in the long run.'

'The Kent story wasn't a lie,' she said baldly.

'No?'

'No. I had agreed to act as co-respondent so that he could get his wife to divorce him, and in return I was to have enough money to start my brother on an artistic career and get away from my detestable home and start a life of my own.'

There was a short pause after this unsteady rush of words. Then Clive said:

'So you came up to London yesterday with the idea of joining him?'

'Yes.'

'You had instructions to go out and enjoy yourself until

this afternoon, when—by the mercy of Providence and no credit to him—he summoned you and informed you he had changed his mind?'

'No, it wasn't quite like that.'

'But substantially correct?'

'I suppose so. First of all I saw him and he seemed very glad I'd come. He——Well, anyway, that doesn't matter now. Then I went out early this evening to meet my brother. I was not going to tell *him* how I got my money, of course, but I was going to give him everything he needed—so that he wouldn't have to stay at the office he hated any more. And then I found he didn't need me—it—at all. Some famous artist had seen his work and was taking an interest in him. He was going to do far more for him than I ever could have done. My chief reason for running away just didn't exist any more.'

'That was pretty hard luck,' commented Clive.

'Yes. Only, of course, it *was* lovely that Richard should have such a chance.'

'Of course.'

'I tried to be pleased and happy about that, and I determined to carry out my part of the bargain, anyway. But when I got home—*she* had been.'

'She?'

'His wife.'

'Oh yes. Ginette Darnley, isn't she? A very engaging lady, I should imagine,' he said sarcastically.

'I didn't see her. Not this time, I mean, though I knew her slightly. But they'd had a long talk and decided to patch things up and start again. *He* didn't need me either. He wanted to give me a few hundred pounds, just to square things up, I suppose, and so that I need not go back home, but could stay here and train for a job. I wouldn't take the money as a present, but I agreed to take it as a loan, and I walked out of the house there and then.'

'The wisest action you've performed in the last two days, Virginia.'

She smiled faintly, but Clive remained quite serious.

'You know you've had a remarkably lucky escape, don't you?'

She had not thought of it quite that way, and she stirred uneasily.

'Are you shocked?'

'Oh, Lord, no. I'm not shocked. I'm only profoundly relieved that you came here to a safe friend like Jessica and——What did you tell Jessica originally, by the way? The secretary version?'

'No. I told her I was going to—well, to live with him, but I said it was a genuine love affair. That was what the world was to think, of course.'

'Of course. And poor old Jessica represented the deluded world?'

Virginia nodded. 'More or less.'

'Did she swallow the story?'

'I think so. She seemed to find it difficult to believe that anything so sophisticated as Jason Kent would fall in love with me.'

'But not specially strange that you should fall in love with him?'

She didn't answer, only stared and stared into the fire, where she saw the clearest picture of Jason Kent looking at her with puzzled, dark eyes.

The glowing coal shifted in the grate, there was a shower of sparks, and the picture was gone. But before she could collect her thoughts for a reply, Clive said quietly:

'Oh, I see. I'm sorry. I didn't realise there was that complication, too.'

Characteristically, he made no further comment at all. After a pause he simply asked:

'What are the plans for the future, Virginia?'

'I'm not quite sure. I haven't even begun to think about them.'

'Well, I should if I were you.' He was kind but quite firm about that. 'There's nothing like a definite future plan for piercing together a shattered world again.'

Virginia looked at him and smiled bravely.

'Yes, I'm sure you're right about that. I think I'll start training to-morrow for the sort of secretarial job you're all so sure I couldn't hold down.'

'That's the idea. You could hold one down all right with proper training and experience, of course. Have you anything towards it at all?'

She shook her head doubtfully.

'I don't know a scrap of shorthand or anything about typing.'

'It doesn't matter. They'll teach you all that at the place I have in mind.'

'*You're* going to help me to find a place to train?'

'Of course. You didn't think I was going to leave you stranded, did you?'

'Oh, you're so good! I don't know how——'

'Nonsense. Do you know any languages?'

'Yes. My French is very good—I do know that. Aunt Julia thought it an accomplishment suitable even to my useless position, so it's no special credit to me that I was taught it very thoroughly.'

'God bless Aunt Julia, then. She has her points. Now the question of where you're going to live.' Clive seemed perfectly capable of working out her whole scheme of life for the future in this cheerful manner. And he was right about one thing—it did help enormously to have something definite in view. 'I don't know if——' he began. And then at that moment Jessica's key sounded in the door.

'Hello! Are you still here? I'm awfully sorry——' She came into the room and stopped dead. '*Virginia!*'

'Yes. I—you said——'

'Things haven't turned out quite as Virginia expected,' Clive explained casually. 'So, very wisely, she came back here. I've given her some supper and she feels better now. But I expect what she wants most of all is to go to bed. You can put her up all right, can't you?'

'Of course.' Jessica took command of the situation at once. 'You can sleep on the settee quite easily, Virginia, and tomorrow we'll see about some better arrangement. And you run along now, Clive. We don't need you and, anyway, it isn't decent to have you hanging about an unattached female's flat at this time of night. The phone call didn't come through, of course, did it?'

'No.' Clive got up quite good-temperedly at his dismissal. 'I remembered afterwards. It was *tomorrow* she was going to phone. So sorry I kept you here on false pretences.'

'No, don't be sorry.' Clive spoke rather seriously. 'I'm very glad that you did.' Then he turned to bid Virginia goodnight. 'Now, sleep well. Don't worry about anything. And tomorrow I'll look in and see about taking you to this business college I mentioned.'

'Thank you.' She took his hand in nervous, grateful fingers. 'I can't really thank you, of course, but you know how I feel, don't you?'

'Yes. That's all right. Goodnight, Virginia.'

'Goodnight, Clive.'

He nodded to his cousin, who returned the casual salutation in kind, and then he went off to his own flat.

Jessica, in her turn, asked singularly few questions, considering the circumstances. While she was busy making up a bed on the studio settee, she just said:

'Have you left him for good?'

'Oh, yes.'

'Before anything drastic happened?'

'There was nothing drastic in the sense you mean. He

just changed his mind and his wife is coming back.'

'Well, I won't pretend I don't think it's for the best. I do.'

'I dare say you're right,' sighed Virginia.

'I am, really. Though, of course, it isn't how one looks at these things at the time.'

'No.'

'Did I hear Clive say something about your starting tomorrow on a business training course?'

'Yes.'

'That's fine. It'll take your mind off things.'

'Yes, I know. Besides, I've got to live, and I want to use the money I have sensibly.'

'Naturally.' Jessica flicked sheets and thumped pillows with great energy. 'If you liked the idea of staying around here, I think there's a bed-sitting-room free just across the landing from here. You could share my bathroom—and the kitchen, too, if you liked. We could probably have some of our meals together, and there'd be a gas-ring in your own room for snacks when we got tired of each other's company.'

'Oh Jessica you are indeed an angel! I don't know why Clive and you are so good to me.' Virginia felt near tears again.

'Oh, nonsense! We're not *so* exceptional. But we're quite nice when we're roused,' Jessica admitted. 'Now you just make yourself comfortable and go to bed. Good-night— and sleep well. And remember that no unhappiness lasts for ever and very few of them for as long as six months.'

Long after Jessica had gone, Virginia lay thinking over the strange events which had been packed into the last two days.

The terrible, urgent ache of misery was gone for the time. Not finally conquered, she was afraid, but at least temporarily lulled, and her thoughts travelled thankfully backwards and forwards over the goodness of her two new friends.

They were right. She could—and would—build her life afresh. In a sense, she had a great chance in front of her— the means to make some sort of decent, if undistinguished, career, safe from the tyranny of her aunt. It was more than she had deserved, and it was for her to make a success of it.

The light grew fainter and her thoughts more indistinct. What was it Clive had said?—that she had had a very lucky escape? From what—from what?

From Jason Kent, she supposed.

But only a few weeks ago she had thought that he himself represented escape. Jason, with his mocking, disturbing way of talking, his tired, rather cynical eyes which brightened when he looked at her, his imperious demands, his strange flashes of feeling.

How much had she romantically imagined about him?— and how much was the truth?

She fell asleep still trying to find the answer.

CHAPTER NINE

AFTER that evening, there began for Virginia an entirely new and strangely satisfying life.

She found, to her relief and delight, that secretarial school was not beyond her. She was at least as good as the others round her, and in some respects she was unquestionably their superior. The fact restored her confidence and self-respect in a way that she could hardly have credited.

Here was something she could really do. All the discipline and daily grind of Aunt Julia's rule helped her rather than hindered her here. She was used to hard work—expected it and never resented it, particularly now that it was for a set purpose.

And such a purpose! One day she was to be independent and self-supporting. And it would not be a distant day either.

Her day-to-day arrangements with Jessica worked with almost perfect smoothness. They saw enough of each other, but not too much, and the friendship deepened and took on an added intimacy.

Virginia—who had to be at the college at an hour when Jessica liked to be crawling reluctantly from bed—always had her breakfast in her own room. But, by the time she came home in the evening, Jessica had had enough of her own company, and the two girls nearly always had their evening meal together.

Then sometimes, if neither of them was going out, Virginia would come and study quietly in the studio, while Jessica worked or read. And, more often than not, Clive would drop in to have a cup of coffee with them and report on his day's activities.

Sometimes he would take one or other of them out for the evening—sometimes both. But in everything there was a free and pleasant informality which Virginia thought the loveliest way of living she had ever known.

She saw something of Richard during this time, though he was very much absorbed in his own affairs. They met in Town and had a meal together, fairly soon after Virginia had started on her business training.

'I don't wonder you didn't hold that first job down, Virginia,' he remarked, with the frankness permitted only to brothers. 'After all, you hadn't any real qualifications.'

'No.' Virginia agreed. 'That was the trouble.'

'I know—I've had some of it. Office life is hell unless you really know something about it, and then it's a hell of boredom.'

'Thanks for the encouragement,' Virginia said.

'Oh, well—' Richard laughed. He laughed so much more easily nowadays, she noticed thankfully. 'I dare say it will suit you, Jinny. If you honestly like this grind at the business school, I suppose you'll like the other, too. I was just the complete square peg in a round hole, no doubt. But I'm awfully happy now.'

'I'm so glad. It makes me happy just to hear you say that.'

He came once to the studio and obviously liked Jessica as a person very much.

Once Virginia went up to the big house overlooking Wimbledon Common, and had tea with Richard in his very comfortable rooms.

She even had the extreme happiness of meeting the famous David Parkington for the space of five minutes. But the opportunity was rather wasted on her, because she kept on thinking of Jason's remarkably accurate description— 'an indescribably self-satisfied person in a large hat.' As the meeting took place in the garden, even the large hat was in evidence.

However, he quite obviously had something like a genuine liking for Richard, and Virginia felt there was no reason for her to pass criticism on someone who had been so good to her brother.

In a modified way he approved of her, too, it seemed.

'One day I must paint your sister,' he observed to Richard as though she were not there. 'It's an unusual face. The bone structure is remarkable.'

Then, evidently under the impression that he had transported her to the seventh heaven of delight, he took his departure.

Richard's observation was:

'I suppose you *are* rather good-looking, Jinny. I hadn't thought of you that way before.'

Virginia supposed that for so much at least she should be grateful to David Parkington.

It was on this same occasion that Richard said:

'By the way, Jinny, I've had a letter from Aunt Julia. She seems quite honestly under the impression that you're living in sin with Jason Kent. I suppose she can't *help* being an idiot about these things.' Richard was more tolerant in these happier days. 'I don't expect you want to write to her even now, but I think I might. Shall I tell her you left the place long ago and she's got the whole thing wrong?'

'If you like.' Virginia spoke rather curtly.

'I'd like to tell her she was completely wrong about something,' Richard said reflectively. 'Besides, I see no harm in letting her know there *is* nothing between you, and never was. No need for her to think of you as a scarlet woman when you're not.'

'No, I suppose not.'

'All right,' Richard finished cheerfully, having settled the matter to his satisfaction. 'I'll tell her you only stayed a day or two and have never set eyes on him since. Even Aunt

Julia couldn't think there was a love affair concealed in that.'

'No,' Virginia agreed, 'even Aunt Julia couldn't think there was a love affair if she knew the facts.'

And, of course, there never had been, in any sense of the word.

Already time was beginning to slip by in the most extraordinary manner. The daffodils had long ago replaced her favourite crocuses in the parks, and spring was beginning to pass into early summer.

But she heard nothing of Jason Kent.

There was nothing much that she could expect to hear, of course. But always, when her thoughts were not busy with her work or with something that Clive had contrived for her pleasure, she found herself wondering how he was—where he was—what he was doing.

She sometimes even looked through the gossip columns of the papers, in the vague hope that there might be some news of him.

But there never was.

She would not have liked Jessica or Clive even to know that she looked. So far as they were concerned, she had put the whole wretched incident behind her long ago, and faced a satisfactory future with courage and resolution.

Virginia hoped that *was* so. At least she never allowed herself to show that she grieved over the past. But sometimes she felt that some part of her spirit had really died, that evening Jason gave her that cheque and told her to go her own way.

Of course, six months at the business college wrought a considerable change in Virginia. Any shyness or lack of confidence which still remained from the days of repression were covered by a quiet and earnest manner, well calculated to impress an employer.

'A girl who takes her work seriously.' 'No fool—has her mind on her work.' Those were the sort of remarks which were made about her nowadays. And if she were not quite the official phenomenon that these opinions implied, at least she had a remarkably conscientious outlook for a girl of eighteen.

Work was a pleasant, rather than an unpleasant, necessity to Virginia, and she honestly thought that the life she lived now was heaven compared to the days with Aunt Julia.

Without the slightest qualm, the head of her secretarial college recommended her very earnestly to the senior partner of a stockbroking firm in the city. And without the slightest qualm Mr Sackville had engaged her.

Had he not been rather short-sighted, he might perhaps have hesitated, because Mr Sackville had an uneasy feeling that official employees should not be decorative. However, fortunately he really had only a vague idea of her appearance, and so it was decided that on Monday, the third of September, Miss Virginia Baron should join the staff of Sackville and Dundas.

On the Friday, after bidding farewell to the college staff, Virginia came out of the college into the last bit of August sunshine. She felt extraordinarily contented, and her hopes were pleasantly high. At that moment she could have addressed Aunt Julia herself with cordiality.

It was early to go home, and she walked part of the way—up Lower Regent Street and then along Piccadilly. It was a little out of her way, but she enjoyed the pleasant aimlessness of strolling like this.

For a moment she could not recall when it was she had done something like this before. Then she remembered! Her first morning in London, when Clive had found her looking into the shop in Knightsbridge and taken her on a tour of sightseeing.

Dear Clive! SHe wondered what she would have done without him during the last six months. Without Jessica, too, of course, for she was equally good. But Clive was so resourceful, with his perpetually new ideas for occupying her thoughts and for opening out a new world in front of her.

Perhaps that was why the girl who was walking along Piccadilly now was really someone very different from the stunned, unhappy, inexperienced young creature who had walked slowly through the darkness, weeping, the night she had left Jason Kent's house.

Virginia crossed the road and turned up Bond Street.

This was supposed to have a special significance for her. In Richard's opinion she ought to consider it the most important street in London. For here, in one of the private galleries, hung the portrait which David Parkington had painted of her.

She had been simply astounded when she found that the careless remark about painting her one day had really had foundation in fact.

'But of course. I never say anything I don't mean,' the great David Parkington had tolerantly informed her. And so, to Richard's excitement and her own considerable pleasure, she had gone often to the big house in Wimbledon, and sat in the studio there while her portrait was painted.

Now it hung in a gallery in Bond Street, and Richard thought her little less than mad that she had always been too shy to go in to see it for herself.

'But I've seen it in the studio often enough, and I think it's lovely.' she protested. 'I should feel so self-conscious, going into a public place and being caught gazing at my own face.'

'Virginia! You are *hopeless*. As though your face is the important part of it.' Richard refused to mince his words where his hero's work was concerned. 'It's an exceptionally fine example of his work. That's why people go and look at it. Your face is just incidental. Only it's a great honour to have been the model for a portrait like that. One would think you'd *want* to go and see it now it's hung.'

She supposed it would be a good opportunity now. There were not likely to be many people there, for it was getting late—almost tea-time.

A little diffidently she pushed aside the swing-doors and went into the long, cool room of the private gallery.

Actually there was no one else there at all, and she could go round and look at the pictures in undisturbed solitude. She could see the one of herself at the end, but because it seemed faintly indecent to rush there immediately, she went slowly down the room, pausing to look at other pictures which were there.

Several of them—but not all—had been painted by Parkington, and, although she pretended to no particular knowledge of art, she could see why Richard thought him a wonderful being. There was a vividness and richness about his work that gave it a living quality.

'What a good thing he wasn't the sort of artist to do me with a square face and blue hair,' thought Virginia. 'I should have had to put up with it, all the same, or else break permanently with Richard.'

She was standing in front of the portrait of herself now. He had painted her in a white dress, with a brilliantly striped scarf just falling back from her hair. They had had a great deal of difficulty about the set of that scarf, but now Virginia thought that perhaps it had been worth all the fussing and argument.

She was just turning away when suddenly she noticed with interest that, pinned to the frame, was a small square label which said: 'Sold.'

It must have been quite a recent sale. Richard hadn't known anything about it when she had seen him two days ago.

Odd to think of one's portrait hanging in the house of a stranger, looking down for ever on the daily life of some family one would never know. She felt extreme curiosity about the purchaser of the picture, and wondered if she could find out something about the sale.

She looked round, and noticed that an extremely immaculate young man, who obviously belonged to the place, was examining one of the pictures with an attention that suggested he had never seen it before. He evidently had no wish to trouble her, but did not intend that she should be left entirely unguarded. He showed no inclination to address her, however, perhaps because she did not look at all the sort of person who could pay the prices charged in this gallery.

She went over to him, and immediately his absorbed interest in the picture evaporated. He turned to her with a smile which showed he was there for no other purpose than to answer her questions.

'I was very much interested in the Parkington portrait at the end there,' she said. 'I see it's been sold.'

'Oh, yes.' He seemed to discover that, too, for the first time. 'Yes, it was sold yesterday, I think. An extremely fine example of his work.'

'Yes, it is. I specially wanted to see it because it's of myself. I mean—I was the original—the model, whatever you call it.'

The young man thought that in this particular case you hardly called 'it' the model.

'Of course—I can see it now. A very lovely portrait. You must have been pleased.'

'Oh, I was. Pleased that he should want to paint me, and pleased that it should turn out so well.'

'Exactly.'

He was all polite attention, but seemed to think there was little else to say.

'Do you think I might know who bought it? I don't expect the name would convey anything to me, but I should like to know.'

'Well'—he bit his lip rather doubtfully—'we don't usually expect to disclose details of sales to other enquirers, you know.'

'No.' Virginia coloured slightly, perhaps at her own curiosity. 'No, I can quite understand that. I expect I'd better ask Mr Parkington himself. Only I just wondered. It's a funny feeling to know your portrait is going into someone else's house. I felt frankly curious.'

'Thought it might be someone who knows you?'

'Well, no, I don't think it could be.' She laughed. 'I can't think of anyone I know who could afford to buy a picture like that.'

Perhaps it was the laugh that did it. Virginia did not often laugh. When she did, people were rather apt to want to give her whatever she wanted.

'Just a moment,' the young man said. 'I'll go and find out.' And he went away, leaving her standing there, while her own likeness smiled down at her, as though faintly amused at her curiosity.

'Yes. Here it is.' The young man was coming back, holding an open book in his hand. 'Sold yesterday to Mr Jason Kent. To be delivered at the end of the exhibition to his country house in Shropshire.'

'Thank you,' Virginia said, and slowly began to put on her gloves, because she had to do something.

The young man was still mildly interested.

'Was it a friend—or just someone interested in a good David Parkington?'

'I think,' Virginia said, 'that it must have been the artistic side that interested him.'

'Oh, yes, it usually is. Only sometimes a portrait has a personal interest, too.'

'Of course.'

She smiled faintly at the young man, thanked him, and went out into the street again.

Jason had bought her portrait. Jason had walked into that gallery only yesterday and bought the picture of her.

She tried to imagine him doing it. Then she remembered, with an intolerable little ache at her throat, that she had never seen him walking. He must be a tall, commanding figure, she knew. But she could not visualise him leaving his car, crossing the pavement. going into that gallery and seeing her portrait—with pleasure? Pain? Surprise? What?

What had made him buy it? It was an absurd impulse for him to have had. Surely one to cause the most justifiable friction with Ginette? Unless, of course, she had no idea that she, Virginia, had been 'the woman in the case.'

But no, that was impossible. Everything Jason had said pointed to his having explained to Ginette in the most brutal detail.

Then it was deliberately planned in order to make her furious. They had quarrelled again—one of their fearful, cold rows, in which they vied with each other to find hateful things to do.

Oh, she didn't want her portrait used for that! It was a horrible, horrible thought.

It was also a very far-fetched thought, she realised the next moment. Melodramatic and not specially like Jason, now she came to think of it.

Then why buy the picture?

The most obvious explanation of all was that he found it a valuable and attractive work of art, of course. She could imagine that, if for that reason he had an impulse to buy it, he was not the man to be put off because the model was a girl he had once known in rather—rather disconcerting circumstances.

But that hardly disposed of Ginette's reactions.

Virginia didn't feel like walking any more. She hailed a bus at the next stop, and went up on top. There were not many people there, and she sat, isolated, in the front seat, gazing out of the window without seeing the busy street, trying to imagine why Jason, after all these months, should want any sort of reminder of her.

When she reached home, Jessica already had tea ready, with some special cake as a celebration to mark the beginning of Virginia's first job.

'There you are, my dear. Celebration.'

Virginia smiled absently.

'Of what?'

'My dear girl! Of what do you think? One doesn't start on one's first job every day. And though I know to-day isn't exactly the start, at least it marks the definite fact that you'll be a wage-earner next week.'

'Oh, yes, of course. I was just wandering.' Virginia smiled and coloured. She felt ashamed of herself that she had let some romantic trifle, out of the past, displace the very real and important fact which Jessica wanted to celebrate.

'Forgotten all about it, I suppose?' Jessica looked amused as she poured out tea. 'I must say you take everything very calmly in your stride. It's a gift, I suppose.'

'No.' Virginia thoughtfully took her cup of tea from Jessica's hand. 'I don't take everything calmly in my stride. Something happened this afternoon which I can't take calmly at all.'

She had not really meant to tell Jessica, but now it seemed the most reasonable thing to do. She wanted someone else's opinion on the strange thing that had happened.

'Well?' Jessica stopped with a piece of bread and butter suspended, half way to her mouth. 'Don't tell me the job's off, after all.'

'Oh, no, the job's all right.' It seemed singularly unimportant to her at that moment. 'You know the portrait David Parkington did of me?'

'Of course.'

'I went in to see it to-day, Jessica. And it's been sold.'

'Has it really?' Jessica bit her bread and butter then. 'Well, do you mind? You weren't expecting to have it yourself, were you? I bet whoever bought it had to dip pretty deeply into his pocket to do it.'

'The man who dipped into his pocket was Jason Kent.' She hadn't expected her voice to tremble, but it did just a little—when she said his name.

'Jason Kent! Bought your portrait! Whatever for?' Jessica was too much astonished to choose her words.

'That's just it. I don't know.'

'How do you know he did buy it?'

'I asked to man at the gallery who bought it, and he told me.'

Jessica suggested, 'He probably happened to go into the gallery, saw what he considered an excellent picture and than realised it was you. Then he'd think something like: "Lord, how amusing! The original didn't stay with me. But the copy can." '

Virginia was silent, gazing at her friend in dismay, because, for the first time, it did strike her that some such cynical impulse was not out of the question.

'It would be something of the sort,' Jessica declared. 'That and a desire to rile the Darnley woman, with whom he's probably quarrelled violently again by now.'

'Is that your real opinion, Jessica?'

'It is.'

'You—you didn't wrap it up much, did you?'

'No, I didn't mean to. If you were given half a chance, Virginia, you'd imagine that he bought this portrait for some remote romantic reason which you can't fathom. And you'd make yourself wretched and aimless, wondering and wondering what there was that you ought to find out. Isn't that right?'

'I suppose so.'

'Well, don't, love. I don't want to sound hard, and, goodness knows, I hate meddling where it isn't my business. But don't get yourself involved again in a swamp you've struggled out of once. There may be a thousand reasons why he bought that picture. Cynicism, eccentricity, good business, with an idea of selling later when its value rises—anything. But it certainly wasn't sentiment. Or if it was, it was one of those extremely unworthy flashes of it that he doesn't seem able to live up to. You've had some experience of those already, haven't you?'

She had, of course. Every word that Jessica was saying was sound common sense.

She nodded slowly.

'You're just at the beginning of something rather good, you know. It would be a pity not to get the best out of it now. If I were you I'd wash out this business of the picture. It's a pity you ever knew about it. Forget it, Virginia—just as though it had never happened.'

'Yes, I know you're right, really.' Virginia drew a quick sigh. 'That's what I'll do.'

Which was manifestly untrue, of course, and a resolution which she was quite incapable of carrying out.

During the week-end Clive took her out in the car a good deal. Whether Jessica had said anything to him or not, and he wanted to keep her interest engaged, she could not tell. But at least he was at considerable pains to see that her last week-end before she started work should be a happy one.

On Monday morning Jessica actually got up and made breakfast for them both.

'It's an occasion which even I must notice,' she explained. 'And anyway, I expect your hand is trembling so much that you'd only upset the coffee.'

'It's not quite as bad as that,' Virginia smiled.

'Not nervous?'

'Not *very*.'

'Well, anyway, I like to waft you on your way with all good wishes.'

On her way down to the City by Tube, Virginia looked round with a new sort of interest at her fellow-travellers. She was one of them now—a wage-earner herself. Not just someone who was learning how it was done.

The offices of Sackville and Dundas were near the Bank of England, and Virginia, who had already been there for a preliminary interview, found her way without difficulty. And, after the first confusing day, it became a surprisingly simple and straightforward matter to take her place in the general scheme of Sackville and Dundas's office.

There was something new to learn almost every day, and she found that her work was unexpectedly varied. Occasionally she had a certain amount of responsibility thrust on to her, but on the whole Miss Payne, the senior secretary, took most of that, and she was only expected to do what her senior demanded of her. Whatever that was, however, had to be done perfectly.

She discovered that there were half a dozen typists who worked in the big room beyond her own, and who did the routine correspondence and accounts of the firm. Rather noisy and frivolous young people, who spilt a great deal of make-up in front of the glass in the dressing-room, talked at great length about their boy-friends, and not unnaturally referred to the head of the firm as 'Old Saccharine.' But they were friendly, and Virginia got on with them well.

Virginia decidedly liked the atmosphere of the place. It was not quite that of a 'family' business, but very much less formal than any of the big limited companies from which a stream of typists and clerks poured each lunchtime into the restaurant which Virginia patronised.

September and October seemed to pass like a flash. Virginia felt completely at home in her place at the office now, and she and Miss Payne enjoyed a sort of modified friendship which, while it never extended beyond the limits of office hours, added considerably to the general pleasantness of life.

She was really seriously distressed, therefore, when, two and a half months after she had come to the office, Miss Payne appeared one morning obviously feeling very ill.

'It's nothing, really,' she insisted. 'I hate making a fuss. Something disagreed with me, I expect. I'll get over it.'

But she didn't 'get over it.' As the morning went on, Virginia became convinced that she was seriously ill.

At lunch-time she absolutely insisted on accompanying her to the out-patients' department of the nearest hospital. It was not convenient, of course, that they should both be away from the office so long as was necessary to await their turn. But Virginia felt she had been justified when she heard the verdict from a rather self-important young house-surgeon.

Acute appendicitis. No question of her even going home. She was detained in the hospital and would be operated on that afternoon. Could Virginia please give them all particulars for getting in touch with her relatives?

Virginia did her best—discovering then how very little she knew about the older woman personally—and when she had given all the assistance she could, she returned in a taxi to the office, since she was already very late, and went to Mr Sackville's room to report the whole unfortunate occurrence.

'Well, how are we going to manage now?' he asked her after suitable expressions of regret about Miss Payne.

'I'll do my best,' Virginia informed him. 'I'm nothing like as experienced, but I can make a shot at a lot of the things she does. If you won't expect perfect results at first and don't mind my coming and asking you things occasionally, I think I can carry on all right.'

'That's a good girl.' He was profoundly relieved that she didn't seem scared by the disaster. 'I'll let you have one of the clerks to help with the routine work, and we'll just have to manage as best we can.'

'Thank you, that ought to help a lot. Now, there's the question of that conference this afternoon——'

'Oh, yes. Damn it.' Mr Sackville looked dismayed. 'Miss Payne always came to these half-yearly meetings and took notes of everything I required.'

'I expect I could do that,' Virginia suggested soothingly.

'Good. I'm sorry it's not until five-thirty.' Mr Sackville leant back in his desk and frowned in a short-sighted way. 'It means a late evening for you. Will that inconvenience you?'

'No, not at all. I can phone home to say I shall be late. I haven't any engagement that needs cancelling.' Quite obviously she would have cancelled such an engagement cheerfully if necessary.

'Well, thanks very much. I'm extremely obliged. Come in about quarter-past five and I'll take you along with me. It doesn't take more than ten minutes by taxi.'

Virginia promised that she would, and retired to her own room.

She telephoned to Jessica, explaining the circumstances and warning her that she would be late. Then she addressed herself to the task of coping with as much as possible of her own work and Miss Payne's before five-fifteen.

The office where the conference was to be held was a much more palatial place than the business home of Sackville and Dundas. The conference room itself—a finely proportioned room with a great window overlooking the river—was heavily carpeted and very well furnished.

Several other members of the conference had already

arrived, and greeted Mr Sackville with real or well-feigned cordiality, and others came in as they took their seats.

Virginia found that a place had been provided for her with one or two other secretaries and lesser fry, who presumably were there to take the same type of notes for their employers as she was to do for hers. These places were not, of course, at the conference table itself, but at a smaller table under the window.

Everyone seemed to have arrived now except the Chairman himself, and there was a certain amount of fidgeting and desultory conversation and consulting of watches.

The young man sitting next to Virginia asked her if she happened to have a pen, and she was rummaging in her bag to find one when the door opened once more to admit the Chairman.

'I am sorry, gentlemen, to have kept you,' he said as he came forward. Then there was a second's pause. 'I was unexpectedly detained.'

Virginia didn't need to look up. She knew the voice of the Chairman too well. She knew why there had been that slight hesitation in his speech of apology.

The man they had all been waiting for was Jason Kent.

CHAPTER TEN

THE business of the conference began after that, and Virginia told herself it was too late for her to look up. She pretended that, since she must take down every word, there was no excuse for her to raise her head from her work and start gazing round the room—or at anyone in it.

But she had never done anything quite so difficult as take down in shorthand the words that were being said in that deep, abrupt voice she knew so well.

The others had their say from time to time, of course, but Jason's cool tones dominated the meeting. Once he laughed at something that was said—a short, abrupt laugh, but it reminded her of the way he used to laugh sometimes at her.

Why had it happened like this? Why had it happened like this? And yet she would not have missed this chance for the world.

Again it seemed like Fate. That Miss Payne should have been taken ill that very afternoon, and that Mr Sackville should have decided to take *her* to the conference. It was almost uncanny.

Virginia could not have said how long the meeting lasted. She only knew that she had covered many pages of her notebook with shorthand notes. Then at last Jason said:

'Well, I think that's all we have to consider. Does anyone want to raise any other points?'

It seemed that no one did. And with a sigh of relief, half a dozen secretaries closed half a dozen notebooks and silently thanked heaven that no more of their evening was to be wasted.

'Are you quite well again now, Kent?' That was Mr

Sackville enquiring after Jason's health with that air of
spurious geniality which seemed to characterise most of the
personal questions and answers among these people.

'Oh, yes, thanks.'

'We didn't have you with us last meeting.'

'No.'

Virginia looked up then. There was no reason—or possibility—to keep her gaze averted any longer.

He was looking at her. Not with any significance or even
sign of recognition. It was simply that his abstracted, rather
cold gaze rested on her.

She supposed her eyes must have widened with something of the alarm and nervousness she felt. A very faint
smile appeared round his mouth, and he slightly inclined
his head to her.

She saw Mr Sackville's gaze follow his, and then flicker
back in astonishment to Jason Kent again. His expression
said as plainly as any words: 'Do *you* know "our Miss
Baron"?'

But if Jason sensed the question, he ignored it entirely.
And then there was a general scraping back of chairs as the
company rose.

'I wish to God they'd hurry up,' muttered the young man
who had borrowed Virginia's pen. 'I'm going to miss my
six-fifty if they don't.'

'Do we have to wait until they've gone?' she enquired in
a whisper.

'Oh, well—my old man may want to bleat a bit to me
afterwards. I can't very well go until he gives his nod.'

'No, of course not.' She supposed Mr Sackville might
want to 'bleat' a little, too. She would have to wait and see.

Jason was bidding them all good-evening now, and then
with a general nod to the smaller fry (who murmured a
concerted, 'Good-night, Mr Kent') he went into an inner
office.

She watched him cross the room with a passionate interest that none of the others could have shared. He was walking at last—Jason, who had once looked at her with hard, cold eyes.

He limped slightly, she saw. That tightened her throat in a way that made it difficult to swallow. But at least he was walking. It was a triumph that only he and she could appreciate.

Mr Sackville came over to her then.

'Well, thank you very much, Miss Baron. You got all you wanted all right?' He spoke rather as though it were *she* who required notes of the occasion.

'Oh, yes, it wasn't difficult. Mr Kent spoke very distinctly, and it was he who said most of the things you'd want noted.'

'Yes.' He glanced at her with frank curiosity. 'You know Kent?'

There was a moment's hesitation.

'Only slightly. I didn't know that he would even—even recognise me.'

'Oh, he never forgets a face. At least, he says he doesn't. Anyway, he obviously recognised you.'

'Yes,' Virginia said, and didn't offer to add any details of how she had met him.

'A remarkable man. He seems to have made a good recovery, though they said at one time that he was practically finished.' He looked reflective, then seemed to remember there were such things as trains to catch. 'Well, Miss Baron, there's no need for you to stay any longer. Goodnight and thanks again. Yes, yes, Browne, I'm coming.' And with a final nod to her, he went off with another member of the conference who had offered him a lift to Cannon Street.

They were nearly all gone now, and as Virginia put on her coat again, she saw that the young man who wanted to catch the six-fifty was preparing to make a rush for it. He whirled along the corridor in front of her and sprang into the waiting elevator. And, rather than delay him that precious second which might make all the difference, she smilingly shook her head at the waiting elevator attendant, and walked down the three flights of stairs instead.

Most of the people in the other offices had gone home by now, and the big, wide landings that she passed seemed very empty. That was how her mind felt at the moment—very empty after all the busy activity of this most unusual day.

She was surprised she could feel so blank when she had just seen Jason—even had him smile faintly at her. But she supposed there was a certain element of shock about it. By and by her thoughts would start racing, and she would live over again every minute of that scene.

By now she had reached the ground floor, and as she crossed the wide marble hall she was aware that the elevator had reached the ground floor again, too. The gates opened, and suddenly she knew quite well, without looking round, who it was that had stepped from the elevator.

She refused to look round, and she refused to hurry her step. As though nothing in the world were there to trouble her she went out of the big swing doors and down the steps. He must be quite close behind her, she knew, but he would be going to his car, of course.

Without knowing where the street led, she turned unhesitatingly to her right, because she must go somewhere and she must look as though she were going purposefully.

It was a little dark there, and the road turned again almost at once. Once she was round that corner she could hurry. Though really there would be no reason to do so, because he was safe in his car now. If he had seen her—and he must, of course—he probably was only too willing to let her—

'Virginia,' his voice said quietly but imperiously behind her. 'Will you wait a moment, please. I want to speak to you.'

She stopped—more from a physical inability to go on than anything else, and he came up with her. He towered above her in a way she had hardly expected, and she felt all the six months of hard-won sangfroid fall from her.

'What do you want?' It sounded rather like the protest of a sulky child, she thought, when it was out.

'Simply to have a talk with you. Will you come and have dinner with me?'

'No. I'm expected home for dinner.' She was walking on now, and perforce he had to do the same.

'Home?'

'At the apartment where I live.'

'With Jessica Someone-or-other?'

'Yes.' She wanted to tell him it was not his business.

'Well, will you come and have coffee with me? That won't take long, and she will only think you're detained at the conference.'

'No, I don't think so, thank you. If there's really anything you want to say, you can say it here.'

'Except that I find it—a little difficult to walk much, even now,' he said curtly.

She knew he hated having to say that, and was stricken with remorse that she had forced it from him.

'I'm sorry.' She stopped than and faced him. 'I didn't think. But do you really feel there's much we can say to each other?'

He set his mouth in that obstinate, not very good-tempered way.

'I should like to know how you're getting on, and I didn't know we were not on speaking terms.'

She yielded suddenly. She had an idea that if she didn't, he would go on arguing until he dropped.

'All right. I will come and have coffee with you.'

With a relief that he didn't even try to hide, he summoned a passing taxi.

Virginia got in, and, with a curt direction to the driver he followed her. It was the most extraordinary feeling to have him there beside her, in the unlighted intimacy of a taxi-cab. There hadn't seemed to be anything intimate about sharing a taxi with Mr Sackville, but this was very different. She was terribly conscious of his big figure slumped back in the corner, and in the light of the passing lamps she glanced once or twice at his unsmiling face.

'I thought,' she said at last, 'that you would have your car waiting for you—especially if you don't like much walking.'

'It was waiting for me. I sent it home.'

'But why?'

'Because I wanted to follow you.'

There didn't seem to be any answer to make to that, so she was silent. And presently the taxi, which had been driving steadily westward, drew up outside a well-known coffee-house.

Jason was limping rather badly, she noticed, as they went in to the place, and she wanted terribly to put her arm round him.

The very thought frightened her as soon as it had formed, and she angrily drove it into the back of her mind. As they sat down at a secluded table in a corner of the room, her face was extremely grave—one might almost have said grim.

He looked unsmiling enough, too, as he ordered their coffee, and as he leant back in his chair and the light fell rather more on him, she noticed what a lot of grey there was in his hair nowadays.

'So you took up your quarters with the artist friend?' He seemed to remember all the details about her affairs, and he still seemed to think he had a right to ask about them.

'Yes,' Virginia said, 'With Jessica Young. We more or less share an apartment.'

'Let me see—she's the one with the nice cousin who took you sightseeing, isn't she?'

'Yes.'

'And you're very happy there?'

'Oh, yes, they're both most awfully good to me.'

'Both?'

'Clive—the cousin, you know—is always in and out. We see a great deal of him. He's almost like Jessica's brother.'

'Yes, he sounds like somebody's brother.'

'What do you mean by that exactly?' Her colour rose, because she had an idea he was implying some criticism.

'Nothing,' he said disagreeably, 'except that I suppose he's an unusually nice man.'

'I think,' Virginia retorted quietly, 'that he's the very nicest man I've ever met.'

'So? How very satisfactory.' He turned away a little bored to watch their coffee being set on the table.

Virginia gripped her hands together in her lap. She was furious with him. Furious and bewildered. Why did he go to all this bother to get her there if all he wanted was to imply criticism against her friends and make half-sneering remarks to her?

She wished she had the courage to ask him that, but as she had not, she poured out their coffee in silence.

'You must have worked hard in the last six months, Virginia.' That was more conventional and said in a more friendly tone.

'Yes. I went to a good business college. Clive found it for me,' she added—she hardly knew why, except that she had a vague feeling she would like him to know *how* decent and helpful her real friends were.

'He seems invaluable,' Jason observed gravely.

'He is,' she retorted quickly.

'How long have you been with Sackville?'

'Something over two months. I went there at the beginning of September.'

'And you like the place?'

'Very much indeed. I haven't really a very responsible position. But Mr Sackville's secretary was taken ill today, and I think I'm to be allowed to carry on while she's away.'

'And all this is very much more satisfactory than life with your aunt?'

'Oh, yes, of course. I always wanted something like this, and now I have the chance, it's good to find that I can tackle it all right. I think office life suits me. I'm quite different from Richard.'

She hardly admitted to herself why she deliberately drew the conversation a little nearer to the subject of David Parkington, but Jason accepted the opening, presumably without suspicion.

'Oh, yes—the brother. Did everything turn out as he expected?—his fortunes flourishing, too?'

'Yes. He's still living with Mr Parkington. They get on extraordinarily well, and Richard's work is improving enormously. Even I can see that, though I don't pretend to know much about art. Mr Parkington has been very good to Richard.'

'So it seems.'

Jason showed no disposition to elaborate the subject, but stirred his coffee thoughtfully.

'I go there sometimes, of course, and have met him several times.'

'Yes?'

There was a slight pause. And then, cutting through these absurd preliminaries, she came straight to the point.

'Why did you buy his portrait of me?' she asked boldly.

'Eh?' He looked up and frowned then. But the next moment there was a slight, grim smile, rather as a duellist might have smiled when he acknowledged a clever hit. 'Because I wanted it,' he replied coolly. 'A remarkably fine picture, don't you think?'

'Yes, of course.' She was nonplussed. 'I can't imagine why *you* should want it, though.'

'Can't you?' He was much better at this sort of thing than she was. 'You can't permit me an interest in art—or a sentimental desire to commemorate an interesting friendship?'

She was silent. Blankly, coldly silent. She hated the way he said that. It made her realise that Jessica was right: he was more than faintly amused at the whole thing. It was an impulse of sarcastic humour as much as anything else that had made him buy the picture, a cynical whim which he was rich enough to gratify.

'I see.' She had made that feeble rejoinder to him before in equally distressing circumstances, she remembered. And then, in self-defence—as though to show him she was as cool about these matters as he was—she added almost brutally—'I should have thought Mrs Kent would have objected. And with some justification.'

His eyebrows went up.

'Mrs Kent is extremely unlikely to see it,' he said dryly.

'But I thought—the man said you were having it sent home—to your country house.'

'Really, Virginia,' he smiled mockingly, 'you seem to have made very detailed enquiries about this most interesting picture. It's perfectly true that the portrait is now in my country house—it looks very well; you must come and see it one day—but Ginette is very unlikely to see it, since she won't be coming to my house. Neither the country house nor the Town house,' he added explicitly.

'You mean—you mean you've quarrelled again?' That, of course, was not in the slightest degree her business, but then, if he insisted on questioning her so closely, she surely had some sort of right to return the compliment. In any case, this meeting was not of her seeking. It was his own fault if it developed on lines that annoyed him. Especially after that hateful little sneer about her coming to see the portrait. He knew that in no circumstances whatever could she go near his house!

'I suppose "quarrelled" covers it,' he agreed calmly 'Didn't you see that our names figured in the latest list of undefended divorce cases?'

'No.' She caught her breath at that. Not because she was so much surprised, but because it seemed so absurd that one could search and search for news of a person—and then overlook a salient fact published in a newspaper for anyone to see. 'The reconciliation didn't last long, then?'

'No. Reconciliations seldom do, I suppose.'

'Isn't that rather feeble?'

'What?' He looked amused suddenly at her severe tone, and it seemed to her for a moment that she must be sitting on the side of his bed in the magnificent room at his home, scolding him in the half-affectionate, familiar way.

Virginia dropped her eyes, faintly confused at his amusement.

'I only meant that it seems a pity to let yourself get disillusioned and start making cynical generalisations, just because things didn't turn out as you wanted for once.'

There was a slight pause. Then he said gravely:

'I'm sure you're right, Virginia. I accept the rebuke.'

He was laughing at her, she knew, and she said rather curtly:

'I suppose it was a bit—disappointing for you when you had to start all over again. You'd arranged things so well the last time, hadn't you?'

'Oh, yes. But this time it was different. It was I who divorced her.'

He said it so coolly—so exactly as though none of the figures in the case interested him any longer, that Virginia wondered for a moment what she had ever seen in him.

'That was much less trouble, of course.' She was surprised at the quiet steely quality in her voice.

'Oh, much.'

'And much less expensive.'

'Certainly.'

'I don't know,' Virginia exclaimed angrily, 'why we're sitting here saying these cheap and profitless things to each other. It would have been so much better——'

'If I had not insisted on your coming here?' he suggested.

'Exactly.'

'Perhaps you are right. I am sorry my conversation doesn't seem to come up to the standard of the admirable Clive's.'

For a moment Virginia just raised her eyes and looked at him in astonishment. Then, because she was determined that for once he should hear the truth, she spoke very quietly and simply.

'I suppose it's quite impossible for you to understand how much the little everyday kindnesses and sincerity of ordinary people matter,' she said slowly. 'You probably think of anyone like Clive—and Jessica, too—as unimportant and slightly ridiculous. At least, you presume to laugh at them. I'd like you to know that it was their sanity and their normal outlook and their day-to-day kindness that helped me to get things in perspective again and start making a decent life for myself. They're my friends. I love them, and I'm not going to have you sneering at them, simply because you're too blasé and disillusioned even to understand them.'

He made no attempt to interrupt her while she said all this—just leant back in his chair and watched her under those heavy, dark brows of his.

When she had finished, she didn't wait for a reply, but got to her feet, and he perforce had to do the same. He summoned the waitress with a movement of his hand, and Virginia went slowly through the room, without even looking to see that he was following. She felt terribly shaken by what she had said to him, but, in some extraordinary way, relieved too. Now even he must understand.

He paid the bill and followed her into the street.

'It's the sort of life that suits you, Virginia?' he asked.

'Yes. The sort of life that suits me exactly.'

'I see.' It was he who said it that time. 'Will you have a taxi?'

'No, thank you. The Tube will take me just as well. I'll go down here and get it.'

'Very well. I'll take this taxi myself.' He raised his hand, and a passing taxi slid to a standstill.

'Good-bye, Virginia.'

'Good-bye.'

As he got into the taxi, she turned away, running down the steps to the Tube station rather hurriedly.

She was halfway down when she suddenly remembered, with a dismay that shocked the colour from her face, that she had never even bothered to enquire after his health. He had made this magnificent, very difficult recovery, and she, who knew better than anyone what it meant, had not even mentioned it.

She turned back sharply—to the extreme annoyance of a fat, breathless man who was hurrying down behind her—and realised then that, of course, Jason's taxi must have driven off long ago. Besides, how could she go back now and start another series of questions? It was absurd.

When she got in, Jessica already had supper prepared.

'You *poor* thing!' She was full of sympathy. 'I was beginning to wonder if they'd kept you for the night.'

'Oh, no. It was a long conference, that was all.'

She found that she didn't want to tell Jessica about the meeting with Jason. Mean perhaps, because, of course, Jessica had some right to know that her judgment had been correct. But Virginia felt she could not bear very much more.

Fortunately Jessica was much too interested in the story of Miss Payne's sudden illness to make further enquiries about the conference, and any dejection on Virginia's part she put down to very natural fatigue.

'Of course, one's very sorry for the poor woman.' Jessica said cheerfully. 'But it's rather a fine chance for you, if you can take hold of it.'

'Yes. I don't mind the extra work and responsibility. It's an opportunity to handle more than they'd give a junior in the ordinary way. And though, of course, she'll only be away a matter of a month or two, it ought to be long enough to show that they can trust me again in an emergency.'

It was Christmas time before Miss Payne left hospital, and nearly the end of January by the time she returned to the office. By then Virginia was really beginning to feel the strain, and three days after Miss Payne's return, Mr Sackville called her into his office.

'I wanted a word with you, Miss Baron.' He was leaning back in his chair, twiddling his pencil as he always did when he was slightly embarrassed. 'I've been very pleased with the way you pulled your weight while Miss Payne was away, and she tells me she found all her work very satisfactorily in order when she came back.'

'I'm—very glad.' Virginia smiled at him in that way which always reminded him that she was just a little too decorative for his ideas of office life.

'You'll have been with us six months on the third of March, and even in the ordinary way I might have considered the question of a small raise for you then,' Mr Sackville went on. 'But in the circumstances I'm going to date your raise from the next pay day—and I hope you'll find it a little larger than you expected.'

'Oh, thank you!' This time there was a flush as well as the smile. 'I was really very glad to help in any case.'

'Yes, I think you were.' Mr Sackville seemed somewhat amused at the idea of her conventional words actually meaning something. 'Well, I think you've earned a day or two's holiday—I can't make it more at this time of year. If you can arrange it satisfactorily with Miss Payne, I'm quite willing for you to tack three extra days on to a week-end some time soon.'

Virginia thanked him warmly. Then she returned to her own office, to discuss with Miss Payne the possibility of managing the extra days.

'Yes, I don't see why not, if you could do without me for nearly three months, I dare say I could rub along without you for three days,' the other woman agreed with grim humour. 'When do you want to go?'

'Well—I'll think it over, may I? I'm not quite sure what I want to do with it yet.'

'All right. Better perhaps if you don't take the weekend that's just coming along. It will leave us a little more time to get absolutely straight.'

So Virginia agreed, and on the way home, she spent most of the time thinking over alternative schemes for spending her unexpected holiday.

When she reached home there was a telegram waiting for her from Richard.

'*Drink my health. I've won the Enderby Scholarship.*'

'Jessica!' She rushed across to Jessica's flat. 'Here's a telegram from Richard. He's won that scholarship he was crazy about. It means two years abroad! France—Italy— I've forgotten exactly where, but he'll be mad with joy.'

'I should think he's mad already,' said Jessica. 'Why send a telegram when he could have rung you up?'

'Oh, I suppose a telegram is always more dramatic. That appeals to him. He's an awful kid still, you know. Or perhaps he just couldn't get through on the office phone. I've got my raise, by the way.'

'Oh, I'm glad. You deserve it every bit as much as he deserves his scholarship.'

'Oh, I don't know.' Virginia laughed happily. 'He's worked like a slave for this.'

'Well, you've worked like a slave, too. I'm glad someone noticed it.'

'I'm to have three days' leave too—tacked on to a week-end. It will be almost like a week. I'm not sure what I'll do with it. I haven't got past the simple gloating stage yet.' And she went to answer the violent rat-a-tat-tat on the front front door, which announced that Richard had arrived hard on the heels of his telegram.

'Did you get my wire?' She had never seen him so flushed and excited since he was six.

'Of course.' She kissed him. 'A million congratulations!'

'I can hardly believe it. Everything I've ever wanted! Paris in the spring! Italy! I could sit down and howl like a kid.'

'When do you go?' she asked.

'The beginning of next month, I expect—or perhaps the middle.' He was really too much excited to be very accurate. 'I haven't settled anything, of course.'

For a moment he was sunk in happy imaginings. Then he looked up suddenly.

'I'll tell you one thing I've a good mind to do. Go down and see Aunt Julia before I go.'

'Richard! Whatever for?' Virginia was half amused and half dismayed.

'We-ell,' Richard seemed to find it rather difficult to explain himself, 'I suppose it's mostly that when you're so frightfully happy you can afford to be magnanimous. And I'd like——'

'You'd like to go and swank to your aunt, now you've proved yourself,' interrupted Jessica. 'A very human and understandable point of view which there's no need to conceal. Now be honest.'

He laughed.

'I expect there's a bit of that in it, too,' he admitted. 'But I would rather like to see her. I thought once that I hated her and never wanted to see her again. But, of course, you don't go on hating people who haven't the power to make you miserable any longer. She *did* give us a house and home all the while we were kids, Virginia.'

'Yes, of course.' Virginia smiled—a faintly perplexed smile. She was somehow rather touched at this spectacle of a Richard so happy that he loved everyone. But it was odd to hear him talk like that. 'Well, go, by all means, if you want to. In her way, she may be almost pleased to see you.'

'How heart-warming,' remarked Jessica.

'Well, one can't be much more sure of it than that,' Virginia explained. 'It's always difficult to guess just what line Aunt Julia will take. But, since Richard has made a success, Aunt Julia may be very gracious. Anyway, don't let me discourage such a very forgiving and magnanimous outlook.' She smiled at him. 'I know what you mean, I think. You'd like to set out on this marvellous trip at peace with the world.'

'Something like that.' He grinned at her. Then he looked away thoughtfully into the fire. 'I wondered if you'd like to come, too.'

'*I?* But I've not won any scholarship,' Virginia pointed out.

'No, I know. But you're making a success of your job, and, in a way, you've proved yourself too. Besides——'

'The child wants you to go and hold his hand,' Jessica put in shrewdly.

'No, I *don't!* Only of course, it would be much nicer if you did come—and pretty deadly if you don't.'

'Oh, Richard,' Virginia laughed in a troubled way, 'I don't even know that Aunt Julia will allow me in the house.

She probably thinks I'm an up-to-date edition of Jezebel by now.'

'No, no, I wrote and explained.' Richard brushed that aside. 'I bet if we go there in a suitably contrite mood, we shall be forgiven in style.'

'And do you really want that?' Virginia looked at him curiously.

'Well, it sort of straightens things out, doesn't it?'

Virginia laughed at that, and suddenly gave in.

'All right. If you want it so much, I'll come, too. You'd better write to Aunt Julia first and ask if I can come. It would be awkward to get down there and be shown the door at once—and she's quite capable of it. Tell her I'm sorry I left in quite such a hurried way, and I should like to come down now and see her. Don't grovel on my behalf. I don't feel like it.'

'No, of course not!' Richard was shocked at the idea, but youthfully pleased to have gained his point.

'That kid brother of yours is simply priceless,' Jessica observed when he had gone. 'Why does he really want to stir up mud that's settled?'

'Oh, he doesn't think of it like that.' Virginia smiled. 'In a way, he disliked her less than I did, because he didn't have so much of her petty tyranny when he grew up. He thinks it was terribly tiresome and mean of her to have been so blind about his work, but now that everything has worked out all right, he can forget that quite easily. He didn't have the day-to-day misery that made me so sour.'

'You weren't sour! What a ridiculous word to use,' cried Jessica indignantly. 'I bet you're every bit as forgiving as Richard, only you have a good deal more to forgive, as it happens. Besides, as he says, he's so wildly happy just now he could love anyone. You'll be just the same when you have something to be really ecstatic about.'

Virginia smiled again and slightly shook her head. She couldn't think of anything that would engender such a mood of ecstasy that she would really think of Aunt Julia with affection. Unless——

She controlled her thoughts angrily at that point. She also reminded herself that she had many things to make her happy—even if not quite in the wild, excited way that Richard was happy.

And presently Clive came to take her out to the theatre, and she thought with a little rush of tenderness:

'I have *everything* to make me quietly, warmly happy when Clive is so good to me. That's worth a lot more than moments of ecstasy that bring such misery after.'

CHAPTER ELEVEN

RICHARD must have displayed a certain amount of diplomacy and tact in his handling of the correspondence with Aunt Julia, because, in due course, there arrived from her an invitation—couched somewhat in the terms of a Royal Garden Party invitation—which included both himself and Virginia.

The week-end as a whole was hardly a success, but then Virginia had never seen how it could be. Aunt Julia had, rather naturally, not changed much in disposition, and Richard—once the novelty of being approved, for once, at home had worn off—was profoundly bored.

For her part, she was not sorry when the time came for them to return to London, and Richard muttered frankly to her: 'Gosh! I'm glad! Aren't you?'

It said something for his self-control, she supposed, that he had not once sought an opportunity for a conversation with her alone. But, once the rather difficult good-byes had been said, and he and she were on their way again back to the station, perhaps he felt that here was his last opportunity.

'Jinny, I know Aunt Julia has the invention of the Devil, but was there anything at all in this story about you and that chap Kent?'

'A little.'

'I thought there must be. Funny that I never got suspicious before, because, of course, it *was* a bit strange your suddenly arriving in London out of the blue, with everything provided for. I suppose, at the time, I was too excited about my own affairs to use my common sense.'

167

'Perhaps.'

'Did you have an affair with him?' Richard brought that out with great coolness, though she thought he was secretly rather anxious about her reply.

'No, nothing like one,' she assured him.

'Oh, good.' Richard might aspire to a sophisticated view of human relationships, and was extremely fond of saying that 'people's morals were their own affairs,' but he found that when it was a case of his own sister, he felt just as much perturbed and quite as conventional as anyone else.

'You just had a crush on him, I suppose?'

'Well, yes. I never told you at the time, and I think I probably shouldn't have said anything now if Aunt Julia hadn't dug it all up. I *was* mad about him, but he didn't care about me. At the same time, we struck up a—business arrangement in which I could be useful. That was why I left home.'

'I say, do you mean he traded on your being keen on him? That's pretty dirty.'

'Oh, no, no. He didn't know how I felt.'

'I bet he did. Men always know these things.'

'Oh, no, they don't. They're rather stupid about them, as a matter of fact,' Virginia retorted. 'Anyway, Richard, *I* didn't know until almost the last minute.'

'Good lord,' said Richard as though unable to fathom the peculiarities of people in love. 'What happened then? I mean—did you carry off this business deal, whatever it was.'

'No. Circumstances—changed.'

'So the whole thing evaporated?'

'I suppose it did.'

'Then all this fluttering and heart-burning of Aunt Julia is about something that just didn't happen?'

'Exactly.' She said that rather bitterly, and Richard looked at her sharply.

'I suppose you wish it *had*.'

'Richard!' She was half shocked. And then: 'I just don't know,' she added truthfully.

'I suppose you're going to marry Clive, aren't you?'

'I don't know. He hasn't asked me.'

'He will, though. He's a good fellow. I like him.'

'Yes, I know. He's a darling and I'm awfully fond of him. I don't know what I should have done without him during this last year. He's so—kind and—safe.'

'Oh yes, he'd make a good husband. And he thinks the light shines out of you.'

She didn't answer, and after a moment Richard said: 'Do you still see him?'

'Who? Jason?'

'Yes.'

'No. No, of course not. I met him just by chance some months ago. I haven't seen him since.'

Richard cleared his throat.

'I suppose you wouldn't like it if I asked whether you still feel the same about him?'

Virginia smiled faintly at this way of putting it.

'I don't mind. Not since it's you. Somehow, I rather like talking to you about it. For one thing, you don't offer advice. And for another—oh, I suppose we've known each other so long, Richard, that it's rather like discussing it with the reasonable side of myself.'

'Yes—exactly.' He was pleased at the implication.

'I *know* with all the logical part of me that it's absurd even to go on thinking about him. It isn't only that—that he never cared for me. It's partly that he isn't a very worthwhile person. That's why it's silly to go on breaking my heart about him.'

'What did you mean when you say he wasn't a worthwhile person? Did he treat you badly?'

'No. Not badly, exactly. It's just that his whole outlook

is so cynical and unfeeling. He can have a very unkind sense of humour, too. I wouldn't say this to anyone but you, because when other people criticise him I want to get up and kill them. But it's true, and it hurts dreadfully. For instance —it was he, you know, who bought that picture of me——'

'Jolly good taste,' Richard interrupted firmly. 'I don't call that unfeeling.'

'No—but his *reason* for doing it! Just as a cynical reminder of an affair he never quite had.'

'Good lord! Did he say that?'

'Not in so many words. He implied it.'

'Did he?' Her brother looked at her thoughtfully. 'You know, I never believe much in implications. One's apt to jump to wrong conclusions. I think when a man buys a portrait of a girl, at the price one has to pay for a Parkington, the implication—if you want the word—is that he's keen on her.'

Virginia smiled ruefully and shook her head.

'Richard, I'll be quite honest. No one could wish to think that more than I do. No one probably would be more willingly deluded. But it won't work. I wish he cared for me—but he doesn't. That's the simple fact.'

'I see. I'm sorry, Jinny. It's pretty miserable for you.'

'No. A great part of the time I manage not to mope over it. I've lots of other things. My job, and——'

'Good heavens! Only you would find consolation for a broken heart in a typewriter,' declared Richard disgustedly.

The train came in almost at once and they had no further chance of conversation. But Virginia felt in any case that she had said all she wanted to say. And in doing so, she had cleared her own views and seen something like daylight ahead.

It was already fairly late when they reached London, and although Richard took his sister as far as the flat, he refused to come in.

'Good-night, Virginia dear. I'll let you know what the plans are as soon as they're made. And thanks for telling me what you did. I value your confidence, you know.'

It was quite a formal little speech for him, and she was a good deal touched by it.

'Thank you, Richard. I wouldn't have told anyone else half so much,' she said, as she bade him good-night and went into the apartment.

It seemed to Virginia that after that visit to her aunt, and her long conversation with Richard, life really did take on a much quieter and more even rhythm. It was not only that life at the office went very smoothly these days, but her home life seemed to be tending towards what the sentimental could only call 'a happy ending.'

She knew it was only a matter of time now before Clive asked her to marry him. And she knew what her reply was going to be.

Nowadays he was much more apt to take her out on her own, and Jessica very tactfully managed so that there was no necessity to make it a trio. She had a good many friends of her own, both in business and socially, and, as she told Virginia, there was no need to cramp an admirable style.

Virginia laughed, but did not ask her to be more explicit, and events moved on smoothly to a certain evening in late March, when Clive took her to the theatre.

She needed cheering up, he said, because Richard was leaving for the Continent in a few days' time, and, happy though she was at his good fortune, she was going to miss him badly.

They had decided on this outing on the spur of the moment, and managed to get good seats in the circle. Even so, they were a little late, and the play had already begun a few moments when they slipped into their seats.

Even that could not disturb the content of Virginia's mood. She felt happy and carefree and confident. She knew, by that subtle 'something' which there is no identifying, that this was going to be the evening. Before he took her home to the flat that night, Clive would ask her to be his wife.

She was not so madly excited that it took her attention off the play. She could enjoy it quietly and wholeheartedly. And she felt that something in that was symbolical of the life she would have with Clive.

The lights went up for the first interval, and he smiled at her.

'Good, isn't it?'

'The best I've seen for a long time.'

'Yes, I felt that, too. Or else it's just that we're in the mood to enjoy ourselves.'

'It's partly that, too. *I* feel in a mood to enjoy anything to-night.'

'I too.' His eyes lingered on her for a moment.

'Are you going outside for a smoke?'

'No. But shall I fetch you something to drink?'

'Yes, please.' She nodded to him and then turned away to look at the house while he was away.

It was near the end of the run, and the house was not very full. It was all the more remarkable therefore that there was a party in the box almost opposite. Virginia gazed abstractedly at them, thinking how very well-dressed the two women were. The man was distinguished-looking, too. They made a nice group.

And then, as she watched them, the door at the back of the box opened, and Jason Kent came in and joined them.

Just like that. Without any more prelude, and with a suddenness that seemed absurdly dramatic. It was as though she had at last banished him completely from her thoughts, because of what she knew was going to happen that evening, and then he literally walked back into her world.

The ghost she had laid was abroad again.

He never once glanced her way—obviously had no idea of her presence—but she watched every movement of his and could not tear her eyes away. Only when Clive spoke behind her, and she had to turn to take the glass of lemonade he was holding, did she manage to break the spell. And then she felt feverishly anxious that Clive should not notice him.

The lights went down again at last, and Virginia was conscious of a tremendous relief. She need not bother to talk to Clive any more, and she was free to watch Jason again in the faint light from the stage.

At first she didn't even realise the significance of her thoughts having arranged themselves that way. When she did, she was conscious of a cold little shock. Clive—whom she was going to marry—meant nothing at all if Jason were there. He was only a hindrance to her full enjoyment. He ceased to exist when her attention was free for Jason once more.

Oh, it was absurd—an intolerable situation. What did that other man across the gulf of the theatre matter? This was Clive's evening—Clive's and hers. *No* one else should have any significance for her. But she scarcely looked at the stage again. The play had lost its point.

He sat rather far back in the box, so that most of the time she could get little more than an impression of him. But, once, for several minutes, he leant forward into the light, watching the stage in that completely absorbed way he had occasionally looked at her.

Did he look better? It was so difficult to tell in this dim light. Pale, of course, but then he was always that, and as likely as not it was the heavy shadow which made his eyes look large and sleepless.

Anyway, what business was it of hers?

When the second interval came she went outside with Clive. She didn't want to go, but it was the lesser of two evils. If she stayed, Jason might see her, make some sign of recognition, and then Clive would be bound to see. If she went out, she lost precious minutes of watching him— the very few precious minutes when the light was strong enough to see him well.

Clive was talking to her now. She didn't want to listen. But somehow she made the sort of reply she supposed he was expecting.

He was a little troubled, she could see, so she evidently was not doing very well. Something in her manner must have told him the spell was broken. When they went back into the theatre again, he, too, was rather silent.

It was a desperately short act—or so it seemed to her. As though with specially acute senses, she realised just how rapidly the scene was approaching its finale. In ten minutes —in five minutes now—it would all be over. She would not be able to watch Jason any more, and chance might not let her see him again for years.

Years? And what would have happened then?

It was not nervousness that gripped Virginia any longer. It was stark panic. And the cause of it was the pleasant, charming man beside her.

She couldn't marry him. She couldn't, couldn't, couldn't!

She told herself it had nothing to do with Jason—it *could* have nothing to do with Jason, because he hadn't the faintest place in her life. Only she knew that the nicest substitute in the world was useless. Other women might do that sort of thing and make a success of it. She couldn't —that was all. The beginning and end of it.

The performance was over now. He had not even seen her when they stood up to go. And at last there was nothing to do but to turn away and join the slowly moving throng that was going downstairs.

The stairway from the circle led into the main foyer, and

as Virginia and Clive came slowly down the last flight of stairs, Jason and his party stood just below them, putting on coats and wraps.

Deliberately and without a qualm of conscience, she tried to will him to look up at her.

And at that moment he raised his eyes and saw her. He saw Clive, too, of course, for he had her lightly by the arm and was quite obviously escorting her.

The very slightest lift of Jason's eyebrow made the enquiry, and after a second she nodded very faintly in return. He bowed to her then, and that was the first thing Clive noticed.

'Someone you know?' he enquired without much interest.

'Yes,' Virginia said. And then they passed the group and went out of the theatre.

They had to walk a few steps to where the car was parked, and all the time Virginia had her nails dug into her palms. It was over. She could not resign herself to the fact that it was over. Nothing else mattered but that she had passed him and could not go back.

Clive handed her into the car and carefully tucked a rug round her.

'All right?'

'Yes, thank you.' Such a ridiculous travesty of the truth, but that was the sort of thing one had to say.

He drove slowly at first until they were clear of the crowds, and then the speed increased. She had a far-away impression that it was not because he was in a hurry, but because of his suppressed excitement.

She braced herself for what he should say to her. But when it came, it was not at all what she expected.

'What's the matter, Virginia?'

'Nothing.' The conventional untruth slipped out before she could stop it. Then she suddenly thought that at least she need not insult him with that. 'No, that's not quite true. The man who greeted me just now was Jason Kent.'

There was not the slightest sound for a moment, except the hum of the car. Then he said quietly:

'And does just that chance meeting make all the difference?'

'Clive, I'm sorry—more sorry than I can say, but—yes. It wasn't only just now on the stairs. I saw him in the house. I've been watching him all the evening.'

'No, not all the evening, I think. Until the first interval you hadn't seen him, had you?'

'No, that's true.'

'I thought the change came then.'

There was silence again. Virginia wondered what she could say. It was all there, without words—that was the worst of it. And then, because she felt that somehow it was all her fault, she said again:

'Clive, I'm so dreadfully sorry.'

'You have nothing to be sorry about, my dear.'

'Yes, I have. I ought to have known my mind before. I've tried—I've tried——' She couldn't go on to tell him what she had tried to do, but it seemed it was not necessary.

'Yes, I know, you've done your best to forget him. It wasn't your fault that you were wrong in thinking you'd succeeded.'

'I ought—to have realised.'

'No. It was just seeing him that made the difference. Until then you thought the second-best would do, didn't you?'

'Yes.' She spoke faintly.

'And it just won't after all?'

'Clive—I'm sorry. I do know that at least now. It won't do. It would never have done. Whenever this had happened it would have been the same. I suppose at least it was better it should happen now.'

'Yes.'

They didn't say any more after that, and he drove her straight home. As he said good-night to her outside the flat he held her hand.

'Don't worry, Virginia. It couldn't be helped. And it's wonderful even to have you for a friend.'

'That's something I ought to say to you instead, for no one ever had a better friend.' And, leaning forward she gave him a very grave kiss, which he as gravely returned.

Virginia didn't see Jessica until the next morning. But then, as it was Sunday, they both had breakfast together.

It was a little difficult at first, trying to think of casual things to say. But Jessica was not one to stand upon subtle ceremony.

'Well,' she said impatiently, 'haven't you got anything to tell me, as the mothers always said in Victorian stories?'

'Anything to——' Virginia stopped. Then desperately took the plunge. 'I'm not going to marry Clive, if that's what you mean.'

'*Not?*'

'No.'

To her extreme horror and even more extreme astonishment, Jessica burst into tears.

'Jessica!' She had jumped up from the table immediately and in a second was hugging her anxiously. 'What's the matter? I never saw you do such a thing before.'

'No, of course not.' Jessica dabbed her eyes. 'I'm not usually such a fool. Why aren't you going to marry him? Is it because of me?'

'You?' Virginia looked astounded. And then suddenly the truth broke on her. 'Jessica'—she pulled up a chair and sat down rather slowly—'are *you* in love with him?'

'Of course. I've always been in love with him, only he's

got so used to seeing me around that he just takes me for granted, like the telephone and the post and other public services.'

'I—see. What a perfect fool I've been! But why didn't you give me some sort of hint to keep off the grass?'

'Because there wasn't any grass as far as I was concerned. Besides, I thought you wanted him, too, and it was just fair competition—only you started with the advantage.'

'Oh, heavens! I wish I'd known. But, Jessica, the truth is this. It's Jason Kent I love. I can't help what sort of fool you think me—he *is* the only man that matters. I probably shan't ever speak to him again, but that doesn't make any difference. I've got things straight at last. I straightened them out with Clive last night. Next week I'm going to start finding another place to live, because I mustn't contribute to this muddle any longer. And, for heaven's sake, if you love me, do what you can to mend any cracks I've made in Clive's heart.'

'Don't be ridiculous!' Jessica sat up very straight. 'You're not going away from here just because I started snivelling about something that can't be altered.'

'No, it isn't just because of that. And, of course, I'll see a lot of you yourself still. But I'm not going to see Clive for a while. It embarrasses me, it hurts him, and it's darned unfair on you. All I ask is that we use a little common sense and see what happens.'

The point was not settled so easily as that, of course, for Jessica was still strenuously opposing the notion when Virginia returned to her own room. But at least she had won the concession that she should be allowed 'to think things over,' and she spent a good part of that Sunday afternoon reckoning up her resources and deciding on the best re-arrangement to make.

It was while she was doing this and making an intensive study of her finances that she came across the pleasant and surprising fact that her balance at the bank was a good deal more than she had thought.

With a funny, tight little feeling at her heart, she added up the total for the third time.

She had enough to pay back the money she owed him. Once and for all, she could close her account with Jason.

CHAPTER TWELVE

VIRGINIA could not have said exactly when the idea came to her. Some time in the night, she supposed, while she lay in bed, sleepless and worried. But by the time Monday morning dawned, she had made up her mind. She was not going to send a cheque to Jason. She was going to take it to him herself.

What really hardened her resolve in the face of all her nervousness was the fact that she had not actually spoken to him at the theatre—and she *had* to do so once more.

Nothing, of course, was said to Jessica of the absurd idea in her mind. She thought at first she would telephone to say she would be late home from the office, but in the end, she went home instead, and simply said she had to go out later.

It was all quite deliberately planned, and all quite coolly carried out. She never even entertained the thought that he might be out.

After her evening meal she left the flat, taking a taxi because she wanted to arrive calm and unflurried. Her heart was beating now in slow, heavy thumps, but she hardly took any notice of it. Only when the taxi finally stopped with a jerk, her heart seemed to rise in her throat and nearly choke her.

She paid off the taxi and went slowly up the steps. The bell, when she pulled it, sounded with muffled protest somewhere far away in the back of the house, and then she stood there waiting—wondering how she had ever had the courage to come.

It was not a servant she knew who opened the door, and she was glad of that. Only at the last moment had she

180

thought how embarrassing it would be to be recognised and remembered.

She gave her name and asked if she might see Mr Kent.

'Have you an appointment, madam?'

'No,' said Virginia. 'But I think if you'll give him my name he'll see me.'

The servant invited her in, and she sat there waiting in the big, dim hall, while he went away to make enquiries. Presently he returned and asked her to follow him, and she realised she was being led into a part of the house she had not known before.

The man opened a door and, announcing her name, stood aside to let her enter. She went in, and found she was in Jason's study. He got up from a desk as she came in.

'Good evening, Virginia. Won't you come and sit down? What is it I can do for you?'

She heard the door close quietly behind her as she took the chair he offered her.

'Good evening.' For a moment she could think of nothing else to say. Then, opening her bag, she took out the cheque. 'I've brought this for you. It's the money I owe you.'

'The——Oh, yes, of course.' Unexpectedly he flushed as he took it from her. 'Thank you.'

He tossed the cheque almost carelessly on the desk.

'Would you like a receipt? he asked.

'Oh, no, it doesn't matter. Thank you for lending me the money.'

'Not at all.'

They were talking like strangers. This wasn't at all what she had meant to happen. And yet what else could she expect?

It was Jason, as a matter of fact, who first broke away from the conventional business conversation.

'It was a coincidence, seeing you at the theatre the other night. That was——Clive with you, of course?'

'Yes.'

'He looks very nice, Virginia.'

'Oh, he is—very.'

There was a slight pause. Then he said, half turning away to his desk again:

'Am I to give you my very good wishes?'

'About Clive?' She looked almost startled. 'Oh, no. No—certainly not.'

'Not, eh?' He smiled slightly. 'Perhaps I'm premature.'

'Oh, no, there's no question of it.'

'But I thought——Forgive me, it's not my business, of course. I thought I'd never seen a man look more devoted.'

'No—yes, I mean. He is, but—' She stopped.

'But what, Virginia? Why aren't you going to marry Clive?'

'I suppose,' she said slowly, 'one doesn't necessarily love the nicest men best.'

'No. Human nature being the perverse thing it is, I suppose one doesn't. But you haven't really answered my question. Why aren't you marrying Clive, Virginia?'

There was a terrible little silence, and then she said quite crudely:

'You know, don't you? It's because I love you.'

Jason didn't look at her. He was still half turned away to his desk, and his head was slightly bent as he intently drew little pencil designs on his blotting-paper.

'You know I'm years too old for you, don't you?' was the astonishing thing he said.

'I—never thought about your age.'

'Didn't you? It's quite an important factor in these matters. That—and the fact that I'm a sick man, and—what was it you once said?—blasé and disillusioned. It's a poor sum total, Virginia, unless you're going to weigh my money against all that.'

'I never thought of your money either—any more than your age.'

He held out his hand to her.

'Come here to me, my darling,' he said very gently. 'What did you think about, I wonder?'

Virginia came over slowly and knelt down by his chair.

'I thought of *you*,' she said, 'and how I loved you. And I wished you'd love me, only it made no difference even if you didn't. I thought what a hopeless thing pride is—or courage—or anything else when you try to keep from loving someone. And then I just thought that I must come and see you or die.'

He put his arm around her and drew her head down against him.

'Was that what you came to tell me to-night?'

'No. I came to give you back the money, that's all.'

'Oh, yes—the money.' He laughed softly. 'My honest little Virginia—the money!'

'That isn't quite all the truth,' she whispered.

'No, darling?'

'I came just to look at you—to see you smile—or look angry—or any of the things I love.' She turned her face against him and began to cry.

'Don't, my sweet! There's nothing to cry about.' He kissed her hair, and then turned up her face and kissed her wet cheeks and her mouth.

'Isn't—there?' She looked at him doubtfully, her mouth still quivering. 'Aren't you only teasing me? Or do you—do you love me?'

'I love you, my dear. Love you so much that I once did something so gravely out of character that I've been faintly ashamed of it ever since. Magnanimous gestures are not usually in my line,' and he made a slight grimace.

'What—did you do?' Her wide, enquiring eyes were on his face.

'Sent you away, Virginia, for your own good, at a time when I would have given what soul I possessed to keep you with me.'

'Sent me away? *Sent* me away? Do you mean when—when you told me you didn't need me, after all?'

'Um-hm.' His smiling eyes were on her as the truth slowly dawned.

'But why—why—why? I *wanted* to stay. I told you so.'

'Yes, I know. Just as you might have told me that you wanted to commit suicide. But, you see, I'd begun to care what happened to you by then, and I had to do something about it, blasé and disillusioned though I might be.'

'But I don't understand. You were perfectly willing for me to do it right up to——'

'Right up to the time I fell in love with you.'

'And when was that?'

'When you brought me the flowers, Virginia,' he said without hesitation. 'You'd been doing strange things to my heart even before then. But it was then I knew what had happened. When you spent your money—lavishly—just to give me pleasure. You hadn't had much money in your life, had you, my darling? And when you had a little you wanted to spend it on me. It was the strangest, sweetest thing that had ever happened to me.'

'Was it?' She smiled—that slow sweet smile which changed her face so much. 'It seems such a small thing, really. But—I remember—it made me very happy, too.'

He touched her hair very tenderly. Then she glanced up again.

'So you decided to send me away at once?'

'No,' he confessed, 'the idea didn't come as quickly as that. I tell you, noble impulses are not at all natural to me.'

'I think they are.' She reached up and kissed his cheek. 'But go on—tell me.'

'Well, Virginia, I suppose it was while you were talking

about the morning you'd had with Clive. You had obviously
enjoyed yourself so—innocently and so whole-heartedly.
Then you said one odd, rather touching little thing—that it
was the first time you'd really been out with a man. I saw
then vaguely what I was doing with you. I was a little
frightened, though I'm not easily frightened. I realised that
I was taking your life—with your rather naïve permission—
and breaking it into pieces before you could realise the
danger.'

She looked at him very gravely and said nothing.

'Of course you agreed to what I wanted. Of course you
snatched at the chance I'd offered. You simply didn't know
enough about the world to refuse. It was a nasty hour or
two after you'd gone. Especially when I realised that it was
you—who had become inexpressibly dear—whom I had
sacrificed to my callous, uncaring plans.'

'I think—you exaggerate a little.'

'No, dear. Believe me, it was the cold, brutal truth. I'd
been prepared to smash your reputation, upset your sense of
values, and possibly ruin some decent marriage you might
have made later. In return, I was to give you twenty
thousand pounds, because it suited me to do it. I'd never
seen it quite like that before. I went no further than the
shallow idea that your own consent justified it. Only then,
when I cared so frantically what happened to you, did I see
the whole thing in its right colours.'

Virginia leant her head against him once more and looked
very thoughtful.

'And then I came back and told you Richard didn't need
the money?'

'Yes. I'm not a superstitious man, Virginia, but it seemed
to me that if ever anyone had been given a second chance, I
had. I had to invent the idea of Ginette having come on the
spur of the moment——'

'Oh!' She looked up quickly. 'Was that a lie?'

'I'm afraid it was.' He laughed and kissed her. 'Rather a clumsy lie, too, only you were too much upset to see it. It was then that I guessed you already had a romantic attachment for me.'

'But why didn't *that* change things? Why didn't you tell me the truth then? Send me away for a while, if you liked, but tell me the truth first? We could have—have arranged things a different way.'

He frowned and slightly shook his head.

'What sort of a chance would that have been for you? So far as I knew, you already believed yourself half in love with me; you were overwhelmingly sorry for me because I was ill. How could you ever have escaped from all that and taken an objective view—the view I should have wanted you to take if you had just met me later without any of the false elements I'd deliberately introduced? I wanted you to get away clear, Virginia—see for yourself if the ordinary, undemanding, happy things of life were what you needed most. Between your aunt and myself, you'd never had a chance to find out. The only thing was to cut away the whole tangle and send you out free, even if you felt very stunned and wretched at first.'

'It couldn't,' said Virginia, 'have been very easy for *you*.'

'Easy!' He laughed slightly, and then, to her dismay, she felt him shudder. 'No, it wasn't easy. But it was the right thing. And, strangely enough, for the first time in my life, I cared very deeply what the right thing was.'

'Jason, I think if I hadn't loved you before, I should love you now.'

He smiled and drew her close. Then after a while she said thoughtfully:

'So you bought my portrait because you loved me? Funny—Richard was right.'

'Oh—the portrait. Yes, that was a great comfort at first. The poorest substitute—but something. I didn't ever mean to make an attempt to speak to you again, you know. And then when I saw you at the conference the temptation was too much.'

'Oh, Jason! I said some dreadful things to you that evening, didn't I?'

'Well,' he conceded with a smile, 'perhaps it was your turn.'

'Oh, no! And I never asked how you were or anything. I remembered when it was too late and it nearly broke my heart.'

'Never mind. You were very busy telling me what a nice man Clive was, you remember.' He touched her cheek gently. 'Very emphatic you were about that.'

'Oh, how—*stupid*! I remember now—I was hurt and furious because I thought you cynical and uncaring. I think I wanted to hurt you, too—make you see what good friends I really had. It was very petty, wasn't it?'

'No, darling, very human.'

'I think you make too many excuses for me.'

But he shook his head.

Presently she said a little timidly: 'What you told me about Ginette was true, wasn't it? I mean that you have divorced her?'

'Oh, yes.' His complete indifference for a moment reminded her of the old Jason. 'She got involved with some other stage artist. It was simple in the end and, as you remarked, not very expensive.'

'Oh, Jason, I'm so sorry for saying that!'

'Are you?' He laughed. 'I thought it was rather neat at the time, although it stung.'

She kissed him remorsefully then, and he said quietly:

'Are you going to marry me?'

'If you'll have me.'

'No, darling—it's if *you'll* have *me*. I've told you all the disadvantages, but I don't think you listened. I ought to tell you them again, but I can't. I'm so afraid of losing you.'

'You needn't worry,' Virginia told him soberly. 'I did hear what you said, only it didn't mean anything. Reasons and loving someone have really very little to do with each other.'

'Perhaps you're right. I thought, by every argument, you belonged to Clive. A nice, decent fellow who'd built up all the things I'd broken down. It seemed you *must* be his, by some right of conquest.'

But she slowly shook her head.

'It doesn't work like that. Besides, he was several weeks too late. When I met Clive I was already yours, Jason. Yours—with love.'

GREAT LOVE STORIES NEVER GROW OLD...

Like fine old Wedgwood, great love stories are timeless. The pleasure they bring does not decrease through the years. That's why Harlequin is proud to offer...

HARLEQUIN CLASSIC LIBRARY

Delightful old favorites from our early publishing program!

Each volume, first published more than 15 years ago, is an enchanting story of people in love. Each is beautifully bound in an exquisite Wedgwood-look cover. And all have the Harlequin magic, unchanged through the years!

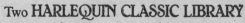

Two **HARLEQUIN CLASSIC LIBRARY** volumes every month! Available NOW wherever Harlequin books are sold.

4 FREE

Harlequin Romances

Your FREE gift includes

- *Anne Hampson* — Beyond the Sweet Waters
- *Anne Mather* — The Arrogant Duke
- *Violet Winspear* — Cap Flamingo
- *Nerina Hilliard* — Teachers Must Learn

FREE GIFT CERTIFICATE

and Subscription Reservation

Mail this coupon today!

In U.S.A.:
Harlequin Reader Service
MPO Box 707
Niagara Falls, NY 14302

In Canada:
Harlequin Reader Service
649 Ontario Street
Stratford, Ontario
N5A 6W4

Harlequin Reader Service:

Please send me my 4 Harlequin Romance novels FREE. Also, reserve a subscription to the 6 NEW Harlequin Romance novels published each month. Each month I will receive 6 NEW Romance novels at the low price of $1.25 each (Total — $7.50 a month). There are no shipping and handling or any other hidden charges. I may cancel this arrangement at any time, but even if I do, these first 4 books are still mine to keep.

_____

NAME   (PLEASE PRINT)

_____

ADDRESS

_____

CITY   STATE/PROV.   ZIP/POSTAL CODE

Offer not valid to present subscribers

Offer expires March 31, 1981   R-2379

Prices subject to change without notice.